The Cultural Fabric Weaves and Unravels

Exploring the Threads that Bind and Unravel Societies

Kemp Porter

Chapter 1: The Historical Threads of Culture

Ancient Civilizations and Cultural Foundations

Ancient civilizations have laid the cornerstone for the rich tapestry of today's cultural landscape. These early societies, with their intricate complexities and variations, set the stage for the evolution of culture as we understand it. From the architectural marvels of Egypt to the philosophical advancements of Greece, each civilization contributed unique threads to the cultural fabric that continues to influence modern societies.

Egypt, often considered one of the cradles of civilization, offers a glimpse into the grandeur of early cultural foundations. Its monumental pyramids, temples, and the enigmatic Sphinx serve as testaments to the Egyptians' architectural ingenuity and their devotion to a complex pantheon of gods. The rituals, hieroglyphics, and art of ancient Egypt were not merely decorative or religious but also carried profound social significance. They reflected the Egyptians' understanding of life, death, and the cosmos, which in turn influenced their social structure and governance.

Meanwhile, across the Mediterranean, the civilization of ancient Greece was burgeoning, leaving an indelible mark on culture, politics, and philosophy. The Greeks introduced democratic principles, fostering a system where citizens could actively participate in governance. This was complemented by their philosophical pursuits, with figures like Socrates, Plato, and Aristotle laying the groundwork for Western thought. The Greek emphasis on reason, inquiry, and the pursuit of knowledge became integral to cultural development. Their contributions in art, theater, and literature have also been significant, with works such as the tragedies of Sophocles and the epic poems of Homer continuing to resonate through the ages.

The influence of ancient Mesopotamia, often referred to as the "cradle of civilization," cannot be overlooked. Situated between the Tigris and Euphrates rivers, Mesopotamia was home to the Sumerians, Akkadians, Babylonians, and Assyrians. It was here that writing first emerged in the form of cuneiform, revolutionizing communication and record-keeping. Mesopotamian innovations in law, mathematics, and astronomy established foundational concepts that are still in use today. The Code of Hammurabi, one of the earliest known legal codes, provides insight into the societal norms and justice systems of the time, influencing subsequent legal frameworks.

The Indus Valley Civilization, with its advanced urban planning and intricate social organization, offers another dimension to our understanding of ancient cultural foundations. The cities of Harappa and Mohenjo-Daro exemplify sophisticated civil engineering, with well-planned streets, drainage systems, and standardized brick sizes. The artifacts and seals unearthed from these sites suggest a complex trade network and a rich tradition of craftsmanship. Despite the mystery surrounding their script, the cultural legacy of the Indus Valley Civilization continues to intrigue historians and archaeologists.

In the Americas, the ancient civilizations of the Maya, Aztec, and Inca each contributed distinct cultural elements. The Maya civilization, known for its advanced knowledge of astronomy and mathematics, developed the concept of zero independently. Their elaborate calendar systems and monumental architecture, such as the pyramids of Chichen Itza, reflect their sophisticated understanding of the world. The Aztecs, with their vibrant capital Tenochtitlan, were renowned for their agricultural innovations, including the use of chinampas or floating gardens. The Inca civilization, spanning the Andes, showcased remarkable feats of engineering with their vast road networks and terraced agriculture, adapting to the challenging mountainous terrain.

Ancient China, with its dynastic cycles, introduced numerous cultural innovations that shaped not only its own society but also those of neighboring regions. The Han Dynasty, for instance, fostered the development of the Silk Road, facilitating cultural and economic exchange between East and West. Confucianism, Daoism, and later Buddhism became philosophical and spiritual pillars, influencing Chinese culture, governance, and social norms. The invention of paper, gunpowder, and the compass during various dynasties further underscored China's contribution to the world's cultural and technological advancement.

Each of these ancient civilizations, through their unique achievements and innovations, contributed to the cultural foundations that have shaped societies across the globe. The exchange of ideas, goods, and technologies among these early cultures established a dynamic interplay that continues to influence contemporary culture. The legacies of these civilizations are evident in modern languages, legal systems, architectural styles, and religious practices, underscoring the enduring impact of ancient cultural foundations.

Cultural Diffusion and Exchange in History

Cultural diffusion and exchange have been pivotal forces throughout history, shaping and transforming societies across the globe. These processes involve the spread of cultural elements—such as beliefs, practices, technologies, and artifacts—from one society to another, often resulting in significant cultural transformations. The movement of people, whether through trade, conquest, or migration, has facilitated the exchange of ideas and customs, enriching the cultural tapestry of civilizations and leaving lasting impacts on the social and cultural landscapes of regions.

The ancient Silk Road stands as one of the most significant conduits for cultural diffusion in history. Extending from China to the Mediterranean, this vast network of trade routes facilitated not only the exchange of goods such as silk, spices, and precious metals but also the transmission of knowledge, religion, and art. The Silk Road connected diverse cultures, allowing for the spread of Buddhism from India to China and beyond. This exchange led to the development of unique cultural forms, such as the fusion of Hellenistic and Indian art in the region of Gandhara, where Greek influences blended with Buddhist iconography to create a distinct artistic style.

The Islamic Golden Age, spanning from the 8th to the 14th century, exemplifies another period of intense cultural exchange. During this time, scholars in the Islamic world preserved and expanded upon the knowledge of ancient civilizations, translating Greek, Persian, and Indian texts into Arabic. The resulting body of knowledge, encompassing mathematics, astronomy, medicine, and philosophy, was later transmitted to Europe, playing a crucial role in the European Renaissance. The Islamic world's position at the crossroads of trade routes facilitated the diffusion of cultural and scientific advancements, highlighting the interconnectedness of civilizations.

In the Americas, the Columbian Exchange marked a significant period of cultural diffusion following the arrival of Europeans in the 15th century. This exchange brought about profound changes in agriculture, cuisine, and ecology, as crops, animals, and technologies were transferred between the Old and New Worlds. The introduction of crops such as potatoes, maize, and tomatoes from the Americas to Europe revolutionized diets and agricultural practices, while the transfer of horses, cattle, and wheat to the Americas transformed indigenous ways of life. Despite the benefits, this exchange also led to devastating consequences, including the spread of diseases that decimated indigenous populations.

The Age of Exploration, driven by European imperial ambitions, further accelerated cultural diffusion. As European powers established colonies across the globe, they encountered a diverse array of cultures and societies. This contact often resulted in the imposition of European cultural norms and practices on colonized peoples, leading to the erosion of indigenous cultures. However, it also facilitated the exchange of ideas, languages, and technologies. In some cases, this interaction led to the emergence of hybrid cultures, as seen in Latin America, where European, African, and indigenous influences merged to create new cultural forms.

The African diaspora, resulting from the transatlantic slave trade, represents another significant aspect of cultural diffusion. Enslaved Africans brought with them a rich tapestry of cultural traditions, including music, dance, religion, and cuisine, which have profoundly influenced the cultures of the Americas and beyond. The blending of African and European cultural elements gave rise to new musical genres, such as jazz and reggae, and religious practices, such as Vodou and Candomblé, which continue to shape cultural landscapes.

Cultural diffusion is not limited to historical events but continues to shape contemporary societies through globalization. The rapid exchange of information, goods, and people in today's interconnected world has led to an unprecedented blending of cultures. This process, while facilitating cultural exchange and understanding, also raises concerns about cultural homogenization and the loss of cultural diversity. The challenge lies in balancing the benefits of cultural diffusion with the preservation of cultural heritage and identity.

Colonization and Its Cultural Impact

Colonization stands as a defining chapter in the annals of human history, leaving indelible marks on the cultural landscapes of both colonizers and the colonized. The process, driven by the pursuit of economic gain, territorial expansion, and the spread of religion, led to profound transformations across continents. This chapter delves into the cultural repercussions of colonization, examining the complex interplay of power, identity, and resistance that shaped societies in its wake.

The arrival of European powers in the Americas, Africa, Asia, and Oceania initiated a wave of cultural imposition. Colonizers often sought to assert their dominance by imposing their language, religion, and social norms on indigenous populations. This imposition was not merely a byproduct of conquest but a deliberate strategy to consolidate power and control. For example, in the Americas, Spanish and Portuguese colonizers enforced Catholicism, seeking to convert indigenous peoples and align them with European cultural values. This religious imposition was accompanied by the suppression of indigenous spiritual practices, leading to a cultural homogenization that erased or marginalized native traditions.

Language played a pivotal role in the colonial agenda, serving as a tool for both control and cultural assimilation. Colonizers introduced their languages as the official means of communication, governance, and education, often at the expense of indigenous languages. This linguistic shift had far-reaching consequences, as language is a cornerstone of cultural identity and worldview. The loss of native languages often led to a disconnection from ancestral knowledge and traditions, as oral histories and cultural narratives were sidelined or lost.

Despite the oppressive nature of colonization, indigenous cultures exhibited remarkable resilience and adaptability. In many cases, colonized peoples found ways to preserve and adapt their cultural practices within the constraints imposed by colonial rule. Syncretism emerged as a response to cultural imposition, resulting in the blending of indigenous and colonial cultural elements to create new, hybrid forms. This is evident in the religious practices of Latin America, where indigenous beliefs and rituals were interwoven with Catholicism, giving rise to unique expressions of faith such as the Day of the Dead and the veneration of syncretic saints.

Resistance to cultural imposition was not only evident in the preservation of indigenous practices but also in the emergence of movements that sought to reclaim and revive cultural identities. The 20th century witnessed a wave of decolonization, as colonized nations gained independence and embarked on efforts to restore cultural heritage and identity. This process, however, was fraught with challenges, as the legacies of colonization continued to influence political, social, and economic structures. Post-colonial societies grappled with issues of identity and belonging, navigating the complexities of cultural hybridity and the desire for authenticity.

The cultural impact of colonization extended beyond the colonized to affect the colonizers themselves. The encounter with diverse cultures often led to a re-evaluation of cultural norms and practices within the colonizing societies. This exchange, albeit unequal, facilitated the flow of ideas, goods, and cultural expressions, contributing to the development of global cultural networks. European art, literature, and philosophy were enriched by the incorporation of exotic themes and perspectives, reflecting the complex interplay of admiration and appropriation that characterized the colonial encounter.

In examining the cultural impact of colonization, it is crucial to recognize the agency of indigenous peoples in shaping their cultural destinies. While colonization imposed significant challenges, it also catalyzed processes of cultural innovation and adaptation. Indigenous artists, writers, and thinkers have played a pivotal role in articulating post-colonial identities, using their work to challenge stereotypes, assert cultural pride, and advocate for social justice. This ongoing dialogue between past and present underscores the dynamic nature of culture and the enduring resilience of human societies.

Today's globalized world continues to grapple with the legacies of colonization, as former colonies navigate the complexities of cultural identity in a post-colonial context. The tensions between cultural preservation and modernization, authenticity and hybridity, remain central to discussions of cultural heritage and identity. By reflecting on the cultural impacts of colonization, we gain insight into the ways in which history shapes contemporary cultural dynamics and the ongoing efforts to reconcile the past with the present.

The Industrial Revolution and Cultural Shifts

The Industrial Revolution, a period of profound technological and economic change that began in the late 18th century, significantly altered the cultural fabric of societies worldwide. This transformation, marked by the shift from agrarian economies to industrialized cities, brought about sweeping changes in every aspect of life, from work and family structures to social norms and cultural expressions. As steam engines powered factories and mechanized production lines, the world witnessed an unprecedented acceleration in urbanization and globalization, laying the groundwork for modern cultural dynamics.

One of the most significant cultural shifts during the Industrial Revolution was the reorganization of society around industrial labor. The rise of factories fundamentally changed the nature of work, drawing people from rural areas to burgeoning urban centers in search of employment. This migration led to the rapid growth of cities, transforming them into hubs of economic activity and cultural exchange. The experience of city life introduced new social dynamics, as individuals from diverse backgrounds converged in cramped living conditions, fostering both a sense of community and social tension.

The industrial workplace itself became a new cultural arena, characterized by regimented schedules and hierarchical structures. The factory system introduced a more rigid division of labor, with workers performing specialized tasks in a repetitive manner. This shift in labor dynamics challenged traditional artisanal practices, where craftsmen took pride in the creation of whole products. The loss of artisanal autonomy and the rise of wage labor led to new class distinctions, with a growing divide between the working class and the industrial bourgeoisie.

Within the confines of industrial cities, cultural expressions began to evolve to reflect the new realities of urban life. The literature of the time, exemplified by the works of Charles Dickens and Elizabeth Gaskell, captured the stark contrasts between wealth and poverty, highlighting the social injustices of the industrial age. Art, too, responded to these changes, with movements such as Romanticism and later Realism providing critiques of industrial society. Romantic artists and writers often idealized nature as a counterpoint to the mechanized world, while Realist works sought to depict the harsh realities of urban existence.

The Industrial Revolution also played a crucial role in shaping gender roles and family dynamics. As men joined the industrial workforce, women often remained responsible for domestic duties, reinforcing traditional gender roles. However, the demand for labor in factories also led to the employment of women and children, challenging existing norms and sparking debates about labor rights and social welfare. The changing roles of women in the workforce contributed to early feminist movements, as women began to advocate for better working conditions and greater social and political rights.

Education and literacy experienced significant advancements during this period, as industrial societies recognized the need for a skilled workforce. The establishment of public education systems provided broader access to learning, empowering individuals with the knowledge and skills needed to navigate the complexities of industrial life. This emphasis on education fostered a more informed populace, capable of critical engagement with social and political issues, and laid the groundwork for the spread of new cultural ideas and movements.

The global reach of the Industrial Revolution facilitated the exchange of cultural influences across continents. As industrial powers expanded their trade networks and colonial empires, they encountered and interacted with diverse cultures, leading to the spread of industrial technologies and the exchange of cultural practices. This interaction was not without conflict, as the imposition of industrial practices often disrupted traditional ways of life, leading to resistance and adaptation by indigenous populations.

Technological advancements during the Industrial Revolution, such as the telegraph and the steamship, revolutionized communication and transportation, shrinking the world and enabling faster exchanges of information and goods. These innovations contributed to the emergence of a global consciousness, as people became more aware of events and cultures beyond their immediate surroundings. The acceleration of communication and travel facilitated the spread of cultural movements and ideas, setting the stage for the interconnected world we inhabit today.

The cultural shifts brought about by the Industrial Revolution continue to resonate in contemporary society. The legacy of industrialization can be seen in the ongoing processes of urbanization, technological innovation, and globalization that define the modern era. As we navigate the challenges and opportunities of this rapidly changing world, the Industrial Revolution serves as a reminder of the profound impact of economic and technological change on cultural dynamics.

Modernity and the Reinterpretation of Tradition

The dawn of modernity brought with it sweeping changes that challenged established traditions and prompted the reinterpretation of cultural norms. As societies transitioned from agrarian economies to industrialized powerhouses, the pace of life quickened, and the world became more interconnected. This period of transformation, characterized by rapid advancements in technology, shifts in social structures, and the rise of new ideologies, compelled individuals and communities to reevaluate their cultural heritage and adapt to new realities.

The concept of modernity is intrinsically linked to the Enlightenment, a movement that championed reason, science, and individualism. Enlightenment thinkers questioned traditional authority and sought to apply rational thought to all areas of human experience, from politics to religion. This intellectual revolution laid the foundation for the modern world, encouraging a departure from tradition in favor of progress and innovation. Yet, even as societies embraced these new ideals, there was a simultaneous effort to reinterpret and preserve cultural traditions, creating a dynamic interplay between the old and the new.

In art and literature, modernity sparked a wave of experimentation that sought to break free from conventional forms and explore new modes of expression. The Impressionist movement in painting, led by artists such as Claude Monet and Edgar Degas, challenged the rigid techniques of the academic tradition, favoring a more spontaneous and subjective approach to capturing light and color. Similarly, in literature, modernist writers like James Joyce and Virginia Woolf pioneered stream-of-consciousness narratives and fragmented structures, reflecting the complexities of contemporary life and the human psyche.

The reinterpretation of tradition was also evident in the realm of architecture. The Industrial Revolution had introduced new materials and construction techniques, prompting architects to reimagine the built environment. The emergence of the Modernist movement in architecture, exemplified by figures like Le Corbusier and Frank Lloyd Wright, rejected ornate historical styles in favor of functionalism and simplicity. This shift was not merely aesthetic; it reflected broader social changes, as architects sought to design spaces that accommodated modern living while addressing the needs of an urbanizing population.

Religious traditions, too, underwent significant transformations during this period. The rise of secularism and the questioning of religious authority led many to reinterpret their spiritual beliefs in light of contemporary knowledge. This reexamination often resulted in the reconciliation of faith with science, as seen in the development of liberal religious movements that embraced scientific advancements while maintaining core spiritual values. At the same time, some communities responded to modernity by reaffirming traditional beliefs, leading to the growth of religious fundamentalism as a counterbalance to secular influences.

The impact of modernity on social structures was profound, particularly in the redefinition of gender roles and family dynamics. The increasing participation of women in the workforce, coupled with the feminist movements of the 19th and 20th centuries, challenged traditional notions of gender and advocated for greater equality. As women gained access to education and employment, the traditional family model shifted, and new forms of domestic arrangements emerged. This reconfiguration of gender roles had lasting implications for cultural practices and social norms, prompting ongoing debates about identity and equality.

Modernity also brought about significant changes in the way societies engaged with their cultural heritage. The preservation of tradition became a conscious effort, as communities sought to protect and celebrate their unique cultural identities in the face of globalization and homogenization. This effort often involved the reinvention of traditional practices to suit contemporary contexts, resulting in a vibrant fusion of the old and the new. Festivals, rituals, and art forms were adapted to reflect modern values while maintaining their historical significance, ensuring their relevance and continuity in an ever-changing world.

The technological advancements of the modern era facilitated the rapid dissemination of cultural ideas and practices, further influencing the reinterpretation of tradition. The advent of mass media, from print to radio to television, allowed for the widespread sharing of cultural content, enabling individuals to access and engage with diverse cultural expressions. This exposure to a multitude of perspectives encouraged cross-cultural dialogue and exchange, leading to the emergence of hybrid cultural forms that blended elements from different traditions.

The reinterpretation of tradition in the context of modernity underscores the resilience and adaptability of culture. While the forces of change prompted by modernity have undoubtedly challenged established norms, they have also provided opportunities for innovation and growth. By reimagining traditions in light of contemporary realities, societies have been able to preserve their cultural heritage while embracing the benefits of progress and globalization.

Chapter 2: Cultural Dynamics in the Modern World

Globalization and Cultural Homogenization

Globalization, a multifaceted process characterized by the increased interconnectedness of economies, societies, and cultures across the world, has brought about significant cultural exchanges and transformations. As goods, services, information, and people move more freely across borders, cultures have become increasingly interwoven, leading to the phenomenon of cultural homogenization. This process, while fostering unity and shared experiences, also raises concerns about the erosion of cultural diversity and the dominance of certain cultural norms.

The rise of globalization has been fueled by advances in technology, transportation, and communication, which have dramatically reduced the barriers to international interaction. The internet, in particular, has played a pivotal role in facilitating the rapid spread of cultural content, allowing people from diverse backgrounds to access and engage with a vast array of cultural expressions. Social media platforms, video streaming services, and online marketplaces have become powerful conduits for the dissemination of cultural products, from music and film to fashion and cuisine.

As global cultural flows intensify, the influence of dominant cultures, particularly those of Western nations, has become increasingly pervasive. The widespread consumption of American movies, music, and fast food, for example, illustrates the reach of Western cultural products and the potential for cultural homogenization. This dominance is often attributed to the economic and political power of Western countries, which enables them to shape global cultural trends and norms. The proliferation of English as a global lingua franca further underscores the influence of Western culture, as it facilitates the dissemination of cultural content and ideas.

While the spread of dominant cultural forms can lead to homogenization, it is important to recognize the agency of individuals and communities in shaping their cultural identities. In many cases, the adoption of global cultural elements is not a passive process but an active negotiation, where local cultures selectively incorporate and reinterpret foreign influences. This dynamic process can result in the emergence of hybrid cultural forms that blend elements from different traditions, creating a rich tapestry of cultural expressions that defy simple categorization.

The impact of globalization on cultural diversity is a subject of ongoing debate. Proponents argue that globalization has the potential to enrich cultures by expanding access to diverse cultural experiences and fostering cross-cultural understanding. The exchange of ideas and practices can lead to innovation and creativity, as individuals and communities draw inspiration from a wide range of cultural sources. Additionally, globalization can empower marginalized cultures by providing them with platforms to share their stories and perspectives on a global stage.

However, critics of globalization caution that the process can lead to the erosion of cultural diversity, as dominant cultural forms overshadow and displace local traditions. The fear is that globalization may result in a homogenized global culture, where unique cultural identities are lost in favor of a standardized set of norms and practices. This concern is particularly acute in the context of indigenous cultures, which often face pressures to conform to dominant cultural models in order to participate in the global economy.

The tension between cultural homogenization and diversity is further complicated by the role of multinational corporations, which often drive the global spread of cultural products. These corporations, in their pursuit of profit, may prioritize marketability over cultural authenticity, leading to the commodification of culture. The commercialization of cultural elements can strip them of their original meaning and significance, reducing them to mere consumer goods.

In response to these challenges, efforts to preserve and promote cultural diversity have gained momentum. International organizations, such as UNESCO, have emphasized the importance of safeguarding cultural heritage and supporting cultural diversity in the face of globalization. Initiatives aimed at protecting indigenous languages, traditional knowledge, and intangible cultural heritage seek to ensure that cultural identities are not lost in the process of globalization.

At a grassroots level, communities around the world are actively working to preserve their cultural traditions and assert their cultural identities. This often involves the revitalization of traditional practices, the documentation of oral histories, and the promotion of cultural education. By engaging with their cultural heritage, communities can foster a sense of pride and belonging while navigating the complexities of a globalized world.

The Rise of Multicultural Societies

Multicultural societies have emerged as defining features of the modern world, shaped by centuries of migration, trade, conquest, and cultural exchange. The rise of these diverse communities reflects the complex interplay of historical forces and contemporary dynamics that have brought people from different backgrounds into shared spaces. This chapter explores the development of multicultural societies, the challenges they face, and the opportunities they offer for fostering cultural richness and social cohesion.

Historically, the formation of multicultural societies can be traced to periods of significant human movement and interaction. The ancient empires of Rome, Persia, and China, for example, were characterized by diverse populations drawn from their vast territories. These empires facilitated the exchange of ideas, goods, and cultural practices, creating cosmopolitan centers where multiple cultures coexisted. In more recent history, the Age of Exploration and the subsequent colonial era saw the movement of people across oceans, leading to the establishment of multicultural communities in the Americas, Africa, and Asia.

The 20th century witnessed a new wave of migration, driven by factors such as economic opportunities, political upheaval, and the aftermath of global conflicts. The aftermath of World War II, in particular, saw significant shifts in population as people sought refuge from war-torn regions or pursued better economic prospects in industrialized nations. These migration patterns have continued into the 21st century, as globalization and technological advancements have made it easier for people to move and communicate across borders.

Multicultural societies are characterized by the coexistence of diverse cultural groups, each with its own distinct language, religion, traditions, and values. The presence of multiple cultures within a single society can enrich the cultural landscape, fostering creativity, innovation, and a deeper understanding of the world. The fusion of different cultural influences can lead to the creation of new cultural forms, as seen in the development of culinary traditions, music, and art that draw from a variety of cultural sources.

However, the rise of multicultural societies also presents challenges, particularly in terms of social integration and cohesion. The coexistence of diverse cultural groups can lead to tensions and conflicts, as differences in values, beliefs, and practices come into contact. Issues such as discrimination, xenophobia, and cultural misunderstandings can hinder the development of harmonious multicultural communities. Addressing these challenges requires a commitment to promoting inclusivity, equity, and mutual respect among all cultural groups.

Education plays a crucial role in fostering understanding and acceptance in multicultural societies. By incorporating diverse cultural perspectives into educational curricula, societies can promote cultural literacy and empathy among individuals. Schools can serve as important spaces for intercultural dialogue, where students from different backgrounds learn to appreciate and respect one another's differences. Language education, in particular, can facilitate communication and bridge cultural divides, enabling individuals to engage more fully in multicultural communities.

Policy frameworks also play a vital role in supporting multicultural societies. Governments can implement policies that promote inclusivity and equality, ensuring that all cultural groups have access to opportunities and resources. Anti-discrimination laws, support for minority languages, and initiatives that celebrate cultural diversity can help create an environment where all individuals feel valued and respected. Additionally, policies that encourage participation in civic life can empower individuals from diverse backgrounds to contribute to the social, economic, and political fabric of society.

Community engagement is another key component of building successful multicultural societies. Grassroots initiatives that bring people together across cultural lines can foster a sense of belonging and solidarity. Cultural festivals, community centers, and intercultural dialogue programs provide opportunities for individuals to share their cultural heritage and learn from others. By creating spaces where cultural exchange is encouraged, communities can build bridges and strengthen social cohesion.

The rise of multicultural societies offers the potential to harness the richness and diversity of human cultures for the benefit of all. By embracing the opportunities presented by cultural diversity, societies can foster innovation, creativity, and resilience. Multicultural societies have the capacity to draw on a wide range of perspectives and experiences, enabling them to adapt to changing circumstances and address complex challenges.

At the same time, the success of multicultural societies depends on the willingness of individuals and communities to engage in ongoing dialogue and reflection. Building inclusive and equitable societies requires a commitment to addressing inequalities and dismantling systemic barriers that prevent full participation. By promoting mutual understanding and respect, multicultural societies can create environments where all individuals feel valued and empowered to contribute to the common good.

Technology's Influence on Cultural Practices

Technology, a driving force behind the evolution of human societies, has profoundly influenced cultural practices throughout history. From the invention of the wheel to the digital revolution, technological advancements have reshaped the ways in which people interact, communicate, and express themselves. The impact of technology on culture is both transformative and multifaceted, affecting everything from daily routines to long-standing traditions, and prompting both adaptation and innovation.

Communication, one of the most fundamental aspects of culture, has been dramatically altered by technology. The advent of the internet and mobile technology has revolutionized how people connect and share information, transcending geographical boundaries and enabling real-time interactions. Social media platforms, blogs, and messaging apps have become integral to modern life, providing new avenues for self-expression and community building. These technologies have democratized access to information and amplified diverse voices, allowing individuals to share their cultural narratives and engage with global audiences.

However, the shift to digital communication has also raised concerns about the erosion of face-to-face interactions and the impact on traditional forms of communication. The immediacy and brevity of digital exchanges can sometimes lead to misunderstandings and a loss of nuance, challenging the depth and quality of human connections. Despite these challenges, technology continues to foster new forms of cultural expression, offering opportunities for creativity and collaboration that were previously unimaginable.

The influence of technology extends to the arts, where digital tools have expanded the possibilities for creation and dissemination. Artists and musicians now have access to a wide range of digital media, from graphic design software to music production tools, enabling them to experiment with new techniques and reach wider audiences. The rise of digital platforms such as YouTube, Spotify, and Instagram has allowed creators to bypass traditional gatekeepers and distribute their work directly to consumers, fostering a more diverse and dynamic cultural landscape.

In the realm of performance arts, technology has enabled immersive experiences that blur the lines between reality and virtuality. Virtual reality and augmented reality technologies offer audiences new ways to engage with performances, creating interactive and participatory experiences that challenge conventional notions of spectatorship. These innovations have the potential to transform cultural practices by introducing new forms of storytelling and audience interaction.

Technology has also influenced the way cultural heritage is preserved and shared. Digital archives, virtual museums, and online databases have made it possible to document and access cultural artifacts and historical records from around the world. These resources provide valuable tools for researchers, educators, and the general public, facilitating the study and appreciation of diverse cultural traditions. Furthermore, digital technologies have enabled the preservation of endangered languages and oral traditions through audio and video recordings, ensuring that these cultural expressions are not lost to future generations.

The rise of e-commerce and digital marketplaces has transformed consumer behavior and the global exchange of cultural goods. Online platforms have made it easier for artisans and small businesses to reach international markets, promoting the cross-cultural exchange of traditional crafts and products. This accessibility has helped to sustain and revitalize cultural industries, providing economic opportunities for communities and fostering appreciation for cultural diversity.

However, the commercialization of culture through technology also raises ethical considerations. The commodification of cultural expressions can lead to issues of cultural appropriation and exploitation, as traditional practices and symbols are used without proper acknowledgment or compensation. It is important for individuals and organizations to navigate these complexities with sensitivity and respect, ensuring that cultural exchange is conducted ethically and equitably.

Education, a cornerstone of cultural transmission, has been transformed by technology through the advent of online learning platforms, virtual classrooms, and digital resources. These tools have expanded access to education and facilitated lifelong learning, enabling individuals to acquire knowledge and skills regardless of their geographic location. Technology has also enhanced the ability to teach and learn about diverse cultures, providing opportunities for cross-cultural understanding and collaboration.

As technology continues to evolve, its influence on cultural practices will remain a dynamic and ongoing process. The integration of artificial intelligence, machine learning, and other emerging technologies promises to further reshape cultural landscapes, offering new possibilities and challenges. The key to harnessing technology's potential lies in fostering a balance between innovation and the preservation of cultural values, ensuring that technological advancements enhance rather than diminish cultural diversity.

The Role of Media in Shaping Cultural Narratives

Media has long been a powerful force in shaping cultural narratives, influencing how societies perceive themselves and the world around them. From the early days of print to the digital revolution of the 21st century, media platforms have evolved, yet their role in crafting and disseminating stories remains central to cultural expression and identity. This chapter delves into the impact of media on cultural narratives, exploring the ways in which it informs, challenges, and reinforces societal norms and values.

The evolution of media began with the advent of the printing press, which democratized access to information and allowed for the widespread dissemination of ideas. Newspapers, pamphlets, and books became vehicles for sharing news, stories, and opinions, shaping public discourse and cultural norms. As literacy rates increased, the written word became a powerful tool for influencing thought, sparking movements and revolutions that transformed societies.

The rise of radio and television in the 20th century marked a new era in media's influence on culture. These platforms brought news and entertainment directly into people's homes, creating shared experiences and collective memories. Radio broadcasts connected listeners to world events in real time, while television introduced visual storytelling that captivated audiences and shaped popular culture. The reach of these mediums allowed for the rapid spread of cultural narratives, from the glamorous portrayals of Hollywood to the political speeches that defined eras.

As media technology advanced, the internet emerged as a transformative force, reshaping how cultural narratives are created and consumed. The digital age has given rise to a multitude of platforms, from social media to streaming services, where individuals can both consume and produce content. This democratization of media production has empowered diverse voices to participate in cultural storytelling, challenging traditional gatekeepers and expanding the range of narratives available to audiences.

Social media, in particular, has revolutionized the way cultural narratives are formed and shared. Platforms like Twitter, Instagram, and TikTok allow users to create and share content with global audiences, fostering a new form of participatory culture. Hashtags and viral trends amplify stories and movements, bringing attention to issues and perspectives that might otherwise be marginalized.

This immediacy and accessibility have made social media a powerful tool for activism and social change, as seen in movements like #MeToo and Black Lives Matter.

However, the proliferation of media platforms has also led to challenges in discerning truth from misinformation. The rapid spread of information, both accurate and misleading, can shape cultural narratives in complex ways, influencing public opinion and societal values. The echo chamber effect, where individuals are exposed primarily to information that aligns with their existing beliefs, can reinforce biases and polarize communities. Navigating this landscape requires critical media literacy, enabling individuals to engage thoughtfully with the content they consume and share.

The role of media in shaping cultural narratives extends to the representation of identity and diversity. Media portrayals influence how individuals and groups are perceived, affecting societal attitudes and behaviors. Positive representation can challenge stereotypes and promote inclusivity, while negative portrayals can perpetuate discrimination and bias. The push for greater diversity in media has led to more inclusive storytelling, offering audiences a wider array of characters and perspectives that reflect the richness of human experience.

In addition to shaping societal norms, media serves as a mirror, reflecting cultural values and historical moments. Documentaries, news reports, and feature films capture the zeitgeist of their times, preserving cultural narratives for future generations. These media artifacts provide insight into how societies understand themselves and their place in the world, offering a lens through which to examine cultural shifts and continuities.

Media's influence on cultural narratives is not limited to the content itself but extends to the ways in which it is consumed. The advent of on-demand content and personalized algorithms has transformed media consumption into a highly individualized experience. This shift has implications for cultural cohesion, as shared experiences become less common and individuals curate their own media environments. However, it also offers opportunities for niche content to thrive, catering to diverse interests and fostering unique cultural communities.

The future of media in shaping cultural narratives will continue to evolve with technological advancements and societal changes. Emerging technologies such as virtual reality and augmented reality offer new possibilities for immersive storytelling, blurring the lines between creator and audience. These innovations have the potential to deepen engagement with cultural narratives, offering interactive experiences that challenge traditional forms of storytelling.

In understanding the role of media in shaping cultural narratives, it is essential to recognize its dual capacity to both reflect and influence society. Media can perpetuate existing power structures or serve as a catalyst for change, depending on how it is wielded. As consumers and creators of media, individuals have the power to shape the narratives that define their cultures, using media as a tool for expression, education, and empowerment.

Cultural Resilience in the Face of Change

Cultural resilience stands as a testament to the enduring strength and adaptability of human societies in the face of change. Throughout history, cultures have encountered myriad challenges, from environmental shifts and political upheavals to technological advancements and globalization. Yet, despite these disruptions, cultural identity and heritage often persist, evolving in response to new circumstances while retaining their core essence. This chapter delves into the concept of cultural resilience, exploring how communities maintain their cultural integrity amidst the forces of change and the strategies they employ to preserve and adapt their traditions.

One of the most profound examples of cultural resilience can be seen in indigenous communities, who have faced centuries of colonization, displacement, and assimilation pressures. Despite these adversities, many indigenous cultures have managed to preserve their languages, spiritual practices, and traditional knowledge systems. Storytelling, oral histories, and rituals play crucial roles in this preservation, serving as vehicles for transmitting cultural values and knowledge across generations. By maintaining these practices, indigenous peoples assert their cultural identity and resist the erasure of their heritage.

Cultural resilience is not merely about preservation; it also involves adaptation and innovation. Communities often reinterpret and modify their traditions to remain relevant in changing contexts. For instance, traditional crafts may incorporate contemporary materials or techniques, blending old and new to create something unique. This adaptability ensures that cultural practices continue to thrive, even as external conditions evolve. By embracing change while honoring tradition, communities can sustain their cultural heritage and foster a sense of continuity.

Education is a powerful tool for enhancing cultural resilience, providing individuals with the knowledge and skills to navigate change while maintaining their cultural identity. Schools and community programs that incorporate culturally relevant curricula and language instruction help to reinforce cultural pride and understanding. By learning about their cultural heritage, individuals are better equipped to engage with the world from a position of strength and confidence, drawing on their cultural roots as a source of inspiration and guidance.

The role of cultural institutions, such as museums, libraries, and cultural centers, is also vital in supporting cultural resilience. These institutions serve as custodians of cultural heritage, preserving artifacts, documents, and art that embody a community's history and values. By providing access to these resources, cultural institutions enable individuals to connect with their past and engage with their cultural identity in meaningful ways. Additionally, these institutions often serve as spaces for cultural exchange and dialogue, fostering mutual understanding and respect among diverse communities.

In the face of globalization, cultural resilience involves finding a balance between embracing global influences and preserving local traditions. The interconnectedness of the modern world offers opportunities for cultural exchange and enrichment, but it also presents challenges to cultural distinctiveness. Communities that successfully navigate this balance often do so by actively participating in the global cultural landscape while remaining rooted in their local heritage. This approach allows them to celebrate diversity and engage with the world without losing sight of their unique cultural identity.

Technology, often seen as a driver of change, can also be harnessed to support cultural resilience. Digital platforms and social media offer new avenues for cultural expression and storytelling, enabling communities to share their narratives with a global audience. Online archives and virtual exhibitions provide access to cultural resources that might otherwise be inaccessible, democratizing the preservation and dissemination of cultural heritage. By leveraging technology, communities can amplify their voices and ensure that their cultural narratives remain vibrant and relevant.

Grassroots movements and community initiatives play a critical role in fostering cultural resilience. Local organizations and networks often lead efforts to revitalize cultural practices, organize cultural events, and advocate for cultural rights. These initiatives empower individuals to take ownership of their cultural heritage and contribute to its preservation and evolution. By building strong community connections and fostering a sense of belonging, grassroots movements create resilient cultural ecosystems that can withstand external pressures.

Cultural resilience also involves addressing the social and economic factors that impact cultural vitality. Access to resources, education, and economic opportunities can significantly influence a community's ability to maintain its cultural practices. Policies that support cultural diversity and inclusion, protect cultural heritage sites, and promote equitable access to resources are essential for fostering cultural resilience. By creating an environment where all communities can thrive, societies can ensure that cultural diversity remains a source of strength and innovation.

Ultimately, cultural resilience is a dynamic process that reflects the interplay between tradition and change. It requires a commitment to honoring cultural heritage while remaining open to new ideas and influences. By fostering a sense of cultural pride and adaptability, communities can navigate the complexities of the modern world with confidence and creativity. Cultural resilience is not only about survival; it is about thriving in the face of change, drawing on the richness of cultural heritage to build a more inclusive and harmonious future.

Chapter 3: Identity and Belonging in a Multi-Cultural Society

The Concept of Cultural Identity

Cultural identity is a multifaceted concept that encompasses the shared values, beliefs, traditions, language, and symbols that define a group of people. It plays a crucial role in shaping individuals' sense of self and belonging, influencing how they perceive themselves and relate to the world around them. Cultural identity is both deeply personal and inherently collective, as it binds individuals to a larger community with a common heritage and history.

At the heart of cultural identity is the notion of belonging. From an early age, individuals are socialized into their cultural environments, learning the customs, norms, and values that are central to their community. These elements provide a framework for understanding one's place within the social fabric, offering a sense of continuity and connection to past generations. For many, cultural identity is a source of pride and strength, offering a foundation upon which to build one's life and make sense of the world.

Language is a fundamental component of cultural identity, serving as both a means of communication and a carrier of cultural meaning. Through language, individuals express their thoughts, emotions, and experiences, while also conveying the values and beliefs of their culture. Language connects individuals to their cultural heritage, preserving stories, traditions, and knowledge that have been passed down through generations. For bilingual or multilingual individuals, navigating multiple languages can enrich their cultural identity, allowing them to engage with diverse cultural perspectives and negotiate complex cultural landscapes.

Traditions and rituals are another key aspect of cultural identity, providing individuals with a sense of continuity and connection to their cultural roots. These practices, which may include religious ceremonies, festivals, and family customs, serve as important markers of cultural identity, reinforcing shared values and fostering a sense of community. By participating in these rituals, individuals affirm their cultural identity and strengthen their bonds with others who share their heritage. The transmission of traditions from one generation to the next ensures that cultural identity remains vibrant and relevant, even as societies change and evolve.

Symbols, such as flags, clothing, and art, also play a significant role in shaping cultural identity. These symbols embody the values and history of a culture, serving as visual representations of cultural identity. They can evoke powerful emotions and serve as rallying points for cultural pride and solidarity. For example, national flags often symbolize a sense of unity and belonging, while traditional clothing can express cultural heritage and individuality. The arts, including music, dance, and visual arts, provide a rich tapestry of cultural expression, reflecting the diversity and creativity of human cultures.

Cultural identity is not static; it is a dynamic and evolving process that is continually shaped by historical, social, and political forces. Migration, globalization, and technological advancements have all contributed to the fluidity of cultural identity, as individuals and communities adapt to new environments and influences. In multicultural societies, individuals may navigate multiple cultural identities, blending elements from different cultures to create a unique sense of self.

The concept of cultural hybridity captures this blending of cultural influences, highlighting the ways in which individuals and communities negotiate and reinterpret cultural identities in response to changing circumstances. Cultural hybridity challenges traditional notions of cultural purity and authenticity, emphasizing the fluid and constructed nature of cultural identity. This perspective recognizes that cultural identity is not a fixed set of characteristics but an ongoing process of negotiation and adaptation.

While cultural identity can be a source of strength and pride, it can also be a site of tension and conflict. Differences in cultural identity can lead to misunderstandings, discrimination, and exclusion, particularly in societies where certain cultural groups hold more power than others. Navigating these tensions requires a commitment to inclusivity and mutual respect, recognizing the value of diverse cultural identities and fostering an environment where all individuals feel valued and respected.

In the face of these challenges, education plays a vital role in promoting cultural understanding and appreciation. Culturally responsive education that incorporates diverse perspectives and experiences can help individuals develop a nuanced understanding of cultural identity, fostering empathy and respect for others. By engaging with diverse cultural narratives and histories, individuals can gain a deeper appreciation for the richness and complexity of human cultures.

Navigating Dual Identities and Hybridity

Navigating dual identities and embracing hybridity has become an increasingly common experience in our globalized world, where individuals often find themselves straddling multiple cultural spheres. This chapter explores the complexities and opportunities that come with living between cultures, examining how individuals construct and negotiate their identities in a world that is constantly shifting and interconnecting.

The journey of dual identities often begins with migration, whether voluntary or forced, as people move across borders in search of new opportunities or in response to external pressures. This movement can lead to the blending of cultural influences, as individuals find themselves navigating the expectations and norms of their host country while maintaining connections to their cultural roots. The intersection of these influences creates a unique cultural landscape where dual identities flourish, allowing individuals to draw from multiple cultural reservoirs.

For many, the experience of dual identity involves a delicate balancing act. It requires navigating the nuances of belonging to more than one cultural group, which can sometimes lead to feelings of dislocation or conflict. On one hand, individuals may feel a strong connection to their cultural heritage, drawing strength and identity from the traditions, language, and values of their ancestral culture. On the other, they may also embrace aspects of the culture in which they currently live, adapting and integrating new customs and practices into their daily lives.

This dual existence can be both enriching and challenging. It offers the opportunity to experience the world through a multifaceted lens, gaining insights and perspectives that are inaccessible to those who identify solely with a single culture. However, it can also lead to internal and external tensions, as individuals may feel pressured to conform to one cultural identity over another or struggle with acceptance from both cultural groups.

The concept of hybridity captures the fluidity and dynamism of navigating dual identities. It acknowledges that cultural identities are not fixed but are instead continuously constructed and reconstructed through interactions and experiences. Hybridity celebrates the blending and intermingling of cultures, recognizing that individuals can create new cultural expressions that reflect their complex identities. This process of cultural synthesis can result in innovative and creative cultural forms, from fusion cuisines and music genres to new social practices and ways of thinking.

One of the key challenges individuals face when navigating dual identities is the pressure to conform to societal expectations and stereotypes. Society often imposes rigid categories for cultural identity, which can limit individuals' ability to express the full complexity of their experiences. For example, someone who identifies as both Mexican and American may feel pressured to choose one identity over the other, depending on the context or the perceptions of those around them. This pressure can lead to feelings of alienation or inauthenticity, as individuals grapple with the tension between personal identity and external perceptions.

To navigate these challenges, individuals can draw on various strategies that affirm and integrate their dual identities. One approach is embracing the concept of both/and rather than either/or, recognizing that it is possible to belong to multiple cultural groups without having to choose between them. This mindset allows individuals to honor and celebrate the diversity of their experiences, recognizing that their identity is enriched by the interplay of different cultural influences.

Storytelling and personal narratives also play a vital role in navigating dual identities. By sharing their stories, individuals can articulate and affirm their unique experiences, fostering understanding and empathy among those who may not share the same cultural background. Storytelling provides a platform for individuals to assert their identities on their terms, challenging stereotypes and misconceptions while highlighting the richness and diversity of their cultural experiences.

Community and social networks are essential sources of support for individuals navigating dual identities. Connecting with others who share similar experiences can provide a sense of belonging and validation, offering a space where individuals can explore and express their identities without judgment. Cultural organizations, affinity groups, and online communities can facilitate these connections, creating opportunities for cultural exchange and solidarity.

Education and cultural awareness also play critical roles in supporting individuals with dual identities. By promoting inclusivity and diversity in educational curricula and programming, institutions can foster environments where all cultural identities are valued and respected. Cultural awareness training and workshops can help individuals and organizations understand and appreciate the complexities of dual identities, promoting empathy and reducing biases.

In embracing hybridity, individuals can become cultural bridges, facilitating dialogue and understanding between different cultural groups. Their unique perspectives allow them to navigate cultural boundaries with ease, fostering connections and building relationships that transcend traditional divisions. As cultural ambassadors, they can contribute to a more inclusive and harmonious society that values the richness of diverse cultural experiences.

The Impact of Migration on Cultural Belonging

Migration has been a fundamental aspect of human history, shaping the cultural landscapes of societies across the globe. As people move from one place to another, they bring with them their customs, traditions, and values, enriching the cultural tapestry of their new homes. However, the experience of migration also raises complex questions about cultural belonging and identity. For many migrants, leaving behind familiar environments and integrating into new ones involves navigating a delicate balance between preserving their cultural heritage and adapting to the cultural norms of their host countries.

One of the most immediate impacts of migration on cultural belonging is the challenge of maintaining connections to one's cultural roots. Migrants often find themselves in environments where their cultural practices, languages, and traditions differ significantly from those of the dominant society. This can lead to a sense of dislocation or cultural loss, as individuals grapple with the reality of being physically distant from their cultural communities. For many, preserving cultural identity becomes an essential aspect of maintaining a sense of belonging, prompting efforts to sustain cultural practices within their new environments.

Language plays a crucial role in the experience of cultural belonging for migrants. It is not only a tool for communication but also a carrier of cultural meaning and identity. Migrants may face the challenge of learning a new language while striving to retain their native tongue, which can create tension between the desire to integrate and the need to preserve cultural heritage. For children of migrants, this linguistic duality can result in a unique cultural identity that blends elements from both their parents' culture and the culture of their new home.

Cultural belonging is also influenced by the social networks and communities that migrants build in their new environments. Forming connections with others who share similar cultural backgrounds can provide a vital source of support and affirmation, helping individuals navigate the complexities of cultural integration. Ethnic enclaves and community organizations often serve as cultural hubs, offering spaces where migrants can come together to celebrate their traditions, share experiences, and maintain a sense of cultural continuity.

The process of cultural adaptation is often accompanied by a negotiation of identity, as migrants reconcile their cultural heritage with the cultural norms and values of their host countries. This negotiation can result in the emergence of hybrid cultural identities, where individuals blend elements from multiple cultures to create a unique sense of self. While this hybridity can be empowering, allowing individuals to draw strength from diverse cultural influences, it can also lead to feelings of ambiguity or conflict, particularly when societal expectations or stereotypes impose rigid categories of identity.

For many migrants, the journey toward cultural belonging involves not only adapting to new cultural environments but also confronting issues of discrimination and exclusion. Prejudice and xenophobia can create barriers to belonging, as migrants may encounter stereotypes or biases that challenge their acceptance within the broader society. These experiences can impact migrants' sense of identity and self-worth, underscoring the importance of fostering inclusive and equitable environments that embrace cultural diversity.

In response to these challenges, many migrants engage in acts of cultural resilience, drawing on their cultural heritage as a source of strength and pride. This resilience is often expressed through the preservation and adaptation of cultural practices, such as traditional cuisine, music, and festivals, which serve as tangible connections to one's cultural roots. By keeping these traditions alive, migrants not only reinforce their own sense of belonging but also contribute to the cultural richness of their host societies.

Education and cultural awareness initiatives play a critical role in facilitating cultural belonging for migrants. Schools and community programs that promote multiculturalism and inclusivity can help create environments where diverse cultural identities are valued and respected. By integrating culturally responsive curricula and fostering cross-cultural dialogue, these initiatives can enhance understanding and appreciation of the diverse cultural contributions that migrants bring to their communities.

The impact of migration on cultural belonging is not limited to the individual level; it also has broader implications for societies as a whole. The cultural diversity introduced by migration can enrich host societies, fostering innovation, creativity, and cultural exchange. However, harnessing the potential of this diversity requires a commitment to inclusive policies and practices that support the integration and empowerment of migrants.

Cultural Identity in the Digital Age

The digital age has ushered in a transformative era for cultural identity, redefining the ways in which individuals express, share, and connect with their cultural heritage. With the proliferation of digital platforms and social media, cultural identity has become both more visible and more complex, as individuals navigate the opportunities and challenges presented by a hyper-connected world. This chapter examines the impact of the digital age on cultural identity, exploring how technology shapes cultural expression, community building, and the preservation of cultural heritage.

The internet serves as a vast repository of cultural knowledge, offering unprecedented access to information and resources about diverse cultures from around the world. Individuals can explore their cultural heritage through online archives, digital libraries, and virtual museums, deepening their understanding of their cultural roots. This access empowers individuals to engage with their cultural identity on their own terms, discovering and rediscovering aspects of their heritage that may have been previously inaccessible.

Social media platforms have become powerful tools for cultural expression, allowing individuals to share their cultural experiences and connect with others who share similar backgrounds. Through platforms like Instagram, TikTok, and Twitter, users can showcase their cultural traditions, share stories, and participate in cultural conversations that transcend geographical boundaries. Hashtags and viral trends amplify these cultural narratives, bringing visibility to diverse cultural identities and fostering a sense of community among users.

The digital age has also facilitated the emergence of new cultural phenomena and expressions, as individuals experiment with blending traditional cultural elements with contemporary digital mediums. Memes, digital art, and online storytelling are just a few examples of how cultural identity is being reimagined in the digital realm. These new forms of cultural expression reflect the dynamic and evolving nature of cultural identity, highlighting the creativity and adaptability of individuals in the digital age.

However, the digital age also presents challenges to cultural identity, as the rapid spread of information can lead to the dilution or misrepresentation of cultural narratives. The internet's vast and decentralized nature can make it difficult to verify the accuracy or authenticity of cultural content, leading to the perpetuation of stereotypes or cultural appropriation. Navigating these challenges requires a critical engagement with digital content, as individuals must discern between genuine cultural expression and content that may distort or exploit cultural identities.

Digital platforms offer both opportunities and challenges for the preservation of cultural heritage. On one hand, the digitization of cultural artifacts, documents, and performances provides a means of preserving and sharing cultural heritage for future generations. Virtual exhibitions and online cultural festivals allow individuals to experience and engage with cultural traditions from anywhere in the world. On the other hand, the transient nature of digital content and the risk of data loss or obsolescence pose challenges to the long-term preservation of cultural heritage.

The digital age has also transformed the way cultural communities are formed and maintained. Online communities and forums provide spaces for individuals to connect with others who share similar cultural backgrounds, fostering a sense of belonging and solidarity. These digital communities can serve as vital support networks, offering a platform for individuals to share experiences, celebrate cultural milestones, and engage in cultural exchange. For diasporic communities, the internet provides a means of maintaining connections to their cultural heritage, even when physically distant from their cultural roots.

Globalization and the digital age have led to an increased blending of cultures, as individuals are exposed to diverse cultural influences through digital media. This cultural exchange can enrich individuals' cultural identities, allowing them to incorporate new elements and perspectives into their cultural expression. However, it also raises questions about cultural authenticity and ownership, as the lines between cultural appreciation and appropriation become blurred in the digital realm.

To navigate the complexities of cultural identity in the digital age, individuals can adopt several strategies that promote authenticity, inclusivity, and respect. Engaging critically with digital content, seeking out diverse and reliable sources, and amplifying marginalized voices are important practices for fostering a nuanced understanding of cultural identity. By supporting platforms and initiatives that prioritize cultural diversity and ethical representation, individuals can contribute to a digital landscape that values and respects all cultural identities.

Education and digital literacy are crucial in empowering individuals to engage thoughtfully with their cultural identity in the digital age. Schools and community programs that incorporate digital literacy and cultural awareness into their curricula can equip individuals with the skills needed to navigate the digital world responsibly. By fostering an understanding of the impact of technology on cultural identity, these initiatives can promote empathy, respect, and cross-cultural understanding.

The digital age offers a unique opportunity for individuals to redefine and reimagine their cultural identity, drawing on the richness of their heritage while embracing the possibilities of the digital world. By engaging with technology in ways that honor and respect cultural diversity, individuals can create a more inclusive and connected global community. This journey of cultural exploration and expression is both personal and collective, reflecting the diverse and interconnected nature of cultural identity in the digital age.

Case Studies of Cultural Integration and Conflict

Cultural integration and conflict are two sides of the same coin, representing the diverse outcomes that can arise when different cultural groups come into contact. Through examining various case studies, we can gain insights into the dynamics of cultural interaction, the factors that foster successful integration, and the challenges that can lead to conflict. These case studies highlight the complexities and nuances of cultural exchange, illustrating that integration and conflict are not mutually exclusive but often coexist in intricate ways.

One illustrative case of cultural integration is the story of Little Italy in New York City, a neighborhood that became a vibrant hub for Italian immigrants in the late 19th and early 20th centuries. As waves of Italians arrived on American shores, they brought with them their customs, language, and culinary traditions. Little Italy served as a sanctuary where immigrants could maintain their cultural identity while adapting to a new environment. Over time, the neighborhood became a melting pot of Italian and American influences, with Italian restaurants and businesses thriving alongside American institutions. The vibrant street festivals and parades that continue today celebrate this cultural fusion, serving as a testament to the successful integration of Italian culture into the broader American tapestry.

In contrast, the experience of the Hmong refugees in the United States presents a case where cultural integration faced significant challenges. Fleeing persecution in Laos after the Vietnam War, many Hmong families resettled in the U.S. during the late 20th century. Upon arrival, they encountered cultural barriers, language difficulties, and economic hardships. The clash between traditional Hmong practices and American societal norms often led to misunderstandings and tensions, particularly in areas such as education and gender roles. Despite these challenges, Hmong communities have persevered, forming tight-knit networks that provide support and preserve cultural heritage. Over the years, efforts to promote cultural understanding and inclusion have facilitated greater integration, but the journey highlights the complexities involved in navigating cultural differences.

Another compelling case study is the integration of Turkish immigrants in Germany, which underscores the interplay of policy and cultural dynamics. Beginning in the 1960s, Germany recruited Turkish workers to fill labor shortages, leading to a significant Turkish diaspora. Initially viewed as temporary "guest workers," many Turks settled permanently, raising questions about cultural integration and identity. The German government's initial reluctance to grant citizenship and equal rights created barriers to integration, contributing to social tensions and cultural isolation. Over time, policy changes and grassroots efforts have sought to address these challenges, promoting cultural exchange and mutual understanding. The younger generations of Turkish-

Germans have largely embraced a dual identity, blending elements of both cultures while advocating for greater inclusivity and acceptance.

The cultural integration of Indian immigrants in the United Kingdom offers a case study of a community that has navigated complex cultural dynamics to achieve remarkable success. Arriving in large numbers during the mid-20th century, Indian immigrants faced discrimination and economic challenges. However, through resilience and community cohesion, they established themselves as a vibrant and influential cultural group. Indian cuisine, music, and festivals have become integral to British cultural life, exemplifying the positive impact of cultural integration. The Indian community's emphasis on education and entrepreneurship has further facilitated their economic and social contributions to the UK, showcasing the potential for cultural diversity to enrich society.

While these case studies highlight successful integration, cultural conflict is an ever-present reality in many contexts. One striking example is the ongoing tension between the indigenous Mapuche people and the Chilean government. The Mapuche, who have inhabited southern Chile for centuries, have faced attempts to assimilate their culture and land by successive governments. The imposition of external cultural norms and economic interests has led to resistance and conflict, as the Mapuche strive to preserve their cultural identity and sovereignty. The struggle underscores the importance of recognizing and respecting indigenous rights and cultural autonomy in fostering harmonious relationships between cultural groups.

The situation of the Rohingya people in Myanmar represents a stark case of cultural conflict with devastating consequences. As a Muslim minority in a predominantly Buddhist country, the Rohingya have faced systemic discrimination and violence, culminating in a humanitarian crisis. The lack of recognition and respect for their cultural identity has fueled conflict and displacement, highlighting the urgent need for international intervention and support. The Rohingya crisis serves as a sobering reminder of the destructive potential of cultural conflict when cultural diversity is not embraced or protected.

These case studies demonstrate that cultural integration and conflict are deeply influenced by social, economic, and political factors. Successful integration often requires deliberate efforts to promote inclusivity, respect for cultural diversity, and equitable access to resources and opportunities. Policies that support multiculturalism and dialogue can facilitate understanding and cooperation between cultural groups, reducing the potential for conflict.

Chapter 4: The Cultural Fabric of Language

Language as a Cultural Pillar

Language serves as a fundamental pillar of culture, intertwining with every facet of human life. It's not merely a means of communication but a vessel that carries the identity, history, and values of a community. Across generations, language has been the thread that weaves individuals into the fabric of their cultural heritage, shaping their worldviews and influencing their interactions with others. Examining the profound role language plays in culture reveals how it acts as both a unifying force and a potential source of division.

At its core, language is the repository of cultural knowledge. It enables the transmission of traditions, customs, and wisdom from one generation to the next. Through stories, proverbs, and oral histories, language preserves the collective memory of a culture, ensuring that its unique identity and experiences endure over time. This transmission is evident in the rich oral traditions of many indigenous cultures, where language serves as the primary medium for sharing histories, beliefs, and practices. These verbal narratives encapsulate the essence of a culture, offering insights into its values and worldview.

Language also shapes human perception and cognition. The linguistic relativity hypothesis, often associated with the work of Benjamin Lee Whorf, suggests that the language one speaks influences how they perceive and understand the world. While the extent of this influence is debated, there is little doubt that language provides the framework through which individuals interpret their experiences. For instance, the presence or absence of specific words in a language can reflect and reinforce cultural priorities and values. In some indigenous languages, there may be numerous terms for different kinds of snow, highlighting the importance of this natural element in their daily lives and survival.

Beyond its cognitive impact, language is a powerful tool for building and reinforcing social bonds. It enables individuals to express their identity and connect with others who share the same linguistic and cultural background. In multicultural societies, language can serve as a marker of community and solidarity, offering a sense of belonging to those who speak it. This is especially true for diaspora communities, where maintaining the native language becomes a crucial way to preserve cultural identity and heritage in a foreign land.

However, language can also be a source of division, particularly in multilingual societies where linguistic differences intersect with issues of power and identity. Language policies and practices can reflect and perpetuate social inequalities, privileging certain languages over others and marginalizing those who speak minority languages. The imposition of a dominant language in educational, governmental, or media contexts can erode linguistic diversity and threaten the survival of minority languages. This dynamic is evident in many post-colonial societies, where indigenous languages have been overshadowed by the languages of former colonizers.

Efforts to preserve and revitalize endangered languages are crucial for maintaining cultural diversity and fostering inclusivity. Language revitalization initiatives often involve documenting and teaching endangered languages, creating resources and materials for language learners, and promoting the use of these languages in various cultural and social settings. Community involvement and empowerment are central to these efforts, as they ensure that language preservation aligns with the needs and aspirations of the speakers themselves.

Technology has emerged as a valuable ally in the fight to preserve linguistic diversity. Digital platforms and tools enable the documentation and dissemination of languages, making resources accessible to a global audience. Language learning apps, online courses, and social media can facilitate language acquisition and practice, connecting speakers across distances and fostering vibrant linguistic communities. However, technology also presents challenges, as the dominance of certain global languages online can further marginalize minority languages.

In addition to its role in preserving cultural heritage, language can be a catalyst for cultural innovation and change. As societies evolve and interact, languages adapt and transform, reflecting new realities and influences. The emergence of pidgins, creoles, and hybrid languages demonstrates the dynamic nature of language as it responds to cultural contact and exchange. These linguistic innovations offer new avenues for cultural expression and identity, showcasing the creativity and resilience of human cultures.

Language also plays a pivotal role in shaping national identity and unity. In multilingual nations, language policies can influence social cohesion and inclusivity. Policies that promote bilingual or multilingual education, recognize multiple official languages, and support linguistic diversity can help bridge divides and foster a sense of shared identity. Conversely, exclusionary language policies that prioritize one language over others can exacerbate tensions and undermine national unity.

For individuals navigating dual identities or living in multicultural environments, language can be both a bridge and a barrier. Bilingualism or multilingualism offers the ability to navigate multiple cultural contexts, drawing from diverse linguistic resources to communicate and connect with others. However, it can also present challenges, as individuals may feel pressure to conform to linguistic norms or face discrimination based on their language proficiency or accent.

The Evolution and Preservation of Dialects

Dialects, as vibrant expressions of cultural identity and regional diversity, offer a window into the linguistic richness of human societies. They are the unique shades and hues of language, reflecting the historical, social, and geographical influences that shape a community. The evolution and preservation of dialects is a captivating journey through time, revealing the interplay between tradition and change, and the efforts to maintain linguistic diversity in an ever-globalizing world.

The evolution of dialects is a natural consequence of language change over time. As communities develop and interact, language adapts to new social realities, environmental conditions, and cultural influences. Dialects emerge as distinct variations of a language, often characterized by differences in pronunciation, vocabulary, and grammar. These variations are shaped by factors such as geographical isolation, historical migration patterns, and cultural exchange, each contributing to the unique linguistic identity of a region.

Historical events play a significant role in the evolution of dialects. Wars, conquests, and trade have historically facilitated the movement of people and the mixing of languages, leading to the emergence of new dialects. The Norman Conquest of England in 1066, for example, introduced Norman French into the English language, significantly influencing its vocabulary and contributing to the development of regional dialects. Similarly, the migration of African slaves to the Americas resulted in a rich tapestry of Creole languages and dialects, blending African linguistic elements with European languages.

The geographical distribution of communities also impacts dialect evolution. Natural barriers such as mountains, rivers, and seas can lead to linguistic isolation, allowing dialects to develop independently over time. The Appalachian dialects of the United States, for example, have preserved many archaic features of English due to the region's relative isolation, providing a fascinating glimpse into the language of early settlers.

Social factors, including class, occupation, and education, further contribute to the differentiation of dialects. In many societies, dialects can serve as markers of social identity, reflecting one's community, background, and even socioeconomic status. This social stratification can result in dialects being perceived as either prestigious or stigmatized, influencing individuals' willingness to use or preserve them in different contexts.

Despite their rich cultural and historical significance, dialects often face challenges to their preservation in the modern world. Globalization, urbanization, and the spread of standardized languages through education and media have led to the decline of many regional dialects. As communities become more interconnected, there is a tendency for dialects to converge towards a standard or dominant language, resulting in the erosion of linguistic diversity.

Efforts to preserve dialects are crucial for maintaining cultural heritage and identity. Language documentation and revitalization initiatives are essential in capturing the unique features of dialects, ensuring they are not lost to future generations. Linguists and community members collaborate to record and analyze dialectal variations, creating dictionaries, grammars, and audio recordings that serve as valuable resources for both academic research and cultural preservation.

Education plays a pivotal role in dialect preservation. Incorporating dialects into the curriculum and promoting their use in schools can foster pride and awareness among younger generations, encouraging them to embrace their linguistic heritage. Bilingual and dialect-inclusive education programs can help bridge the gap between standard languages and regional dialects, providing students with the tools to navigate both linguistic worlds.

Media and technology offer innovative avenues for dialect preservation and promotion. Local radio stations, television programs, and online platforms can showcase dialects, providing a platform for storytelling, music, and cultural expression. Social media, in particular, has become a powerful tool for dialect speakers to connect, share, and celebrate their linguistic identity with a global audience. Hashtags, memes, and viral content can amplify the visibility of dialects, fostering a sense of community and belonging among speakers.

Community engagement and empowerment are at the heart of successful dialect preservation efforts. Grassroots initiatives that involve local speakers in the documentation and promotion of their dialects ensure that preservation efforts are culturally relevant and sustainable. Community festivals, storytelling events, and cultural workshops can create spaces where dialects are celebrated and valued, reinforcing their importance as vital components of cultural identity.

The preservation of dialects is not only about maintaining linguistic diversity but also about honoring the stories, traditions, and identities of the communities that speak them. Dialects carry the echoes of history, the wisdom of ancestors, and the creativity of human expression. By preserving them, we recognize the richness of our shared human heritage and the importance of diverse voices in shaping our collective future.

Language Extinction and Revitalization Efforts

Language extinction is a pressing issue that threatens the cultural diversity and heritage of our world. Languages are disappearing at an alarming rate, with estimates suggesting that nearly half of the approximately 7,000 languages spoken today are at risk of extinction within the next century. This loss is not merely the disappearance of words and grammar but the erasure of entire cultures, histories, and ways of understanding the world. As languages vanish, so too do the unique perspectives and knowledge systems they embody, underscoring the urgency of revitalization efforts.

The causes of language extinction are varied and complex, often involving a combination of social, economic, and political factors. Globalization and the dominance of a few major languages have accelerated the decline of many smaller, indigenous languages. As communities strive for economic advancement and integration into the global economy, there is often pressure to adopt dominant languages for education, employment, and communication, leading to a gradual erosion of native languages. Urbanization and migration also contribute to language shift, as speakers move to cities or different regions, where their native language may not be widely spoken or valued.

Colonization has historically played a significant role in language extinction, as colonizing powers imposed their languages and cultures on indigenous populations. This imposition often involved systematic efforts to suppress native languages through policies that favored the colonizer's language in education, governance, and media. Such historical legacies continue to impact language vitality today, as many indigenous communities struggle to reclaim and revitalize their linguistic heritage in the face of ongoing marginalization and discrimination.

In response to the threat of language extinction, revitalization efforts have emerged as crucial strategies for preserving linguistic diversity and cultural heritage. These efforts encompass a wide range of activities, from documentation and education to community engagement and policy advocacy. Language documentation involves recording and analyzing the linguistic features of endangered languages, creating dictionaries, grammars, and audio recordings that serve as essential resources for revitalization. This work often requires collaboration between linguists and community members, ensuring that documentation efforts are culturally relevant and responsive to the needs of the speakers.

Education is a cornerstone of language revitalization, as it provides opportunities for new generations to learn and use their native languages. Bilingual and immersion education programs have proven effective in promoting language proficiency and cultural pride among young learners. These programs integrate native languages into the curriculum, allowing students to develop literacy and communication skills while also gaining a deeper understanding of their cultural heritage. By fostering a positive attitude toward native languages, education initiatives can help reverse language shift and encourage intergenerational transmission.

Community involvement is vital for the success of language revitalization efforts. Grassroots initiatives that empower local speakers to take ownership of the revitalization process are often the most sustainable and impactful. Community leaders, elders, and language activists play a critical role in promoting language use in everyday life, organizing cultural events, and advocating for language rights. By creating spaces where native languages are valued and celebrated, communities can reinforce their linguistic identity and foster a sense of belonging and pride.

Technology offers innovative tools for language revitalization, providing new platforms for learning, communication, and cultural expression. Digital media, social networks, and mobile applications enable speakers to connect, share, and practice their languages with a global audience. Online resources such as language learning apps, virtual dictionaries, and interactive games can supplement traditional education methods, making language learning more accessible and engaging. However, it is essential to ensure that technology complements, rather than replaces, face-to-face interactions and community-based learning, which are crucial for maintaining the social and cultural dimensions of language.

Policy and advocacy efforts are also critical components of language revitalization. Governments and international organizations can play a significant role in supporting linguistic diversity by recognizing and protecting endangered languages through legislation and funding. Policies that promote the use of native languages in education, media, and public life can help create environments where linguistic diversity is respected and valued. Advocacy campaigns that raise awareness about the importance of language preservation and the rights of minority language speakers can mobilize support and resources for revitalization initiatives.

While the challenges of language extinction are formidable, successful revitalization efforts demonstrate that it is possible to reverse language decline and reinvigorate linguistic communities. The revitalization of the Maori language in New Zealand is a notable example of a comprehensive and collaborative approach to language preservation. Through a combination of government support, community engagement, and educational initiatives, Maori has experienced a resurgence, becoming an integral part of New Zealand's cultural and national identity.

Similarly, the revitalization of the Hawaiian language showcases the power of grassroots movements and cultural pride in language preservation. Despite decades of decline, Hawaiian has been revitalized through immersion schools, cultural programs, and media initiatives, fostering a new generation of speakers and strengthening the cultural heritage of Hawaii.

These success stories illustrate that language revitalization is not only about preserving words and grammar but about empowering communities, celebrating cultural diversity, and fostering resilience in the face of adversity. By embracing the richness of linguistic diversity and supporting revitalization efforts, we honor the voices and stories of countless communities and ensure that the tapestry of human culture continues to thrive for generations to come.

The Influence of Language on Worldviews

Language is not merely a tool for communication; it is a powerful lens through which individuals perceive and interpret the world around them. Each language carries its own unique set of structures, vocabularies, and idiomatic expressions that reflect the cultural and cognitive frameworks of its speakers. The influence of language on worldviews is a fascinating and complex phenomenon, demonstrating the profound ways in which language shapes thought, behavior, and cultural identity.

At the heart of this phenomenon lies the concept of linguistic relativity, which posits that the language we speak influences how we think and perceive reality.

Although the extent of this influence is a subject of ongoing debate among linguists and cognitive scientists, there is compelling evidence suggesting that language plays a significant role in shaping our mental processes. For instance, the way languages categorize color can affect how speakers perceive and distinguish hues. In languages that have multiple terms for shades of blue, speakers are often more attuned to subtle differences between those shades compared to speakers of languages with a single term for blue.

The grammatical structures of a language can also shape its speakers' understanding of time, space, and agency. Consider the concept of time: some languages, like English, use a linear perspective with past, present, and future tenses, which may encourage speakers to perceive time as a sequential progression. In contrast, languages such as Hopi do not use tense in the same way, potentially fostering a more cyclical or holistic view of time. Similarly, languages that emphasize spatial relationships, like Guugu Yimithirr in Australia, which uses cardinal directions rather than left or right, can enhance spatial awareness and orientation skills among their speakers.

Language also influences how individuals attribute causality and agency in events. In English, passive constructions such as "The vase was broken" can obscure the agent responsible for the action, while other languages, like Spanish, more frequently use active constructions that specify the doer, as in "Juan broke the vase." This linguistic difference can affect how speakers assign blame or responsibility, shaping their moral and social judgments.

Beyond cognitive processes, language is deeply intertwined with cultural identity and social norms. It serves as a repository of cultural knowledge, encapsulating the beliefs, values, and traditions of a community. Through language, individuals learn the cultural scripts that guide their behavior and interactions with others. Proverbs, idioms, and metaphors offer insights into a culture's worldview, highlighting what is valued or prioritized within that society. For example, the Japanese concept of "wa," or harmony, is reflected in language through expressions that emphasize collective well-being and social cohesion, underscoring the cultural importance of harmonious relationships.

The influence of language on worldviews extends to the realm of emotions and personal experiences. Different languages offer varying vocabularies for expressing emotions, which can shape how speakers experience and articulate their feelings. The German word "Schadenfreude," describing the pleasure derived from another's misfortune, captures a nuanced emotional experience for which there is no direct English equivalent. Similarly, the Portuguese term "saudade" conveys a deep, nostalgic longing that encompasses both joy and sorrow, highlighting the intricate ways in which language can enrich or limit emotional expression.

The role of language in shaping worldviews is particularly evident in multilingual individuals, who often navigate multiple linguistic and cultural contexts. These individuals may experience shifts in perception and behavior depending on the language they are using, as each language activates different cultural frames of reference. This phenomenon, known as "frame switching," illustrates the fluidity and adaptability of human cognition, as multilingual speakers draw from diverse linguistic resources to construct their understanding of the world.

In multilingual societies, language can serve as both a bridge and a barrier to intercultural understanding. While shared linguistic resources can facilitate communication and cooperation, linguistic diversity can also give rise to misunderstandings and conflict. Efforts to promote multilingualism and linguistic inclusivity can mitigate these challenges, fostering environments where diverse worldviews are respected and valued. Language education programs that emphasize cultural competence and sensitivity can equip individuals with the skills to navigate linguistic and cultural diversity, enhancing their ability to engage with different perspectives.

The interplay between language and worldview has significant implications for global communication and cross-cultural interactions. In an increasingly interconnected world, the ability to understand and appreciate diverse linguistic and cultural perspectives is essential for fostering mutual respect and cooperation. Language learning not only expands one's linguistic repertoire but also opens doors to new ways of thinking and understanding, enriching personal and professional experiences.

Efforts to preserve and revitalize endangered languages are vital for maintaining the rich tapestry of worldviews that linguistic diversity represents. Each language offers a unique lens on the human experience, contributing to the collective knowledge and wisdom of humanity. By supporting language preservation initiatives, societies can honor and celebrate the cultural heritage and identity of linguistic communities, ensuring that diverse worldviews continue to thrive.

Multilingual Societies and Cultural Exchange

Multilingual societies are vibrant mosaics of linguistic diversity, where numerous languages coexist and interact, creating dynamic spaces of cultural exchange. These societies are characterized by the fluidity of communication and the richness of cultural interactions, offering a unique lens through which to explore the interplay of language and culture. As we navigate these multilingual environments, we encounter both opportunities and challenges that shape our understanding and appreciation of cultural diversity.

In multilingual societies, language serves as a bridge that connects individuals across cultural boundaries. It facilitates communication and fosters mutual understanding, allowing diverse groups to share ideas, values, and traditions. The presence of multiple languages within a single community often reflects a history of migration, trade, and cultural contact, where people from different linguistic backgrounds have come together, bringing with them their unique cultural perspectives. This confluence of languages and cultures creates a fertile ground for innovation and creativity, as individuals draw from a diverse pool of linguistic resources to express themselves and engage with others.

One of the most compelling aspects of multilingual societies is the potential for intercultural dialogue and exchange. When people from different linguistic backgrounds come together, they have the opportunity to learn from one another, gaining insights into different worldviews and ways of life. This exchange can lead to a deeper understanding and appreciation of cultural diversity, fostering empathy and respect among individuals. In settings such as schools, workplaces, and neighborhoods, multilingual interactions can create inclusive environments where diverse voices are heard and valued, contributing to social cohesion and harmony.

However, multilingual societies also face challenges that can complicate communication and cultural exchange. Linguistic diversity can sometimes give rise to misunderstandings and miscommunication, especially when language barriers exist. In such contexts, individuals may struggle to convey their thoughts and emotions accurately, leading to frustration and potential conflict. To navigate these challenges, it is essential for individuals to develop language skills and cultural competence, enabling them to communicate effectively and sensitively across linguistic boundaries.

Language policies play a crucial role in shaping the dynamics of multilingual societies. Governments and institutions can influence language use and status through policies that promote or restrict certain languages. For example, official language policies that recognize and support multiple languages can help create equitable environments where all linguistic communities have access to resources and opportunities. These policies can encourage the use of minority languages in education, media, and public life, contributing to the preservation and revitalization of linguistic diversity.

Education is a powerful tool for promoting multilingualism and cultural exchange. Multilingual education programs that incorporate multiple languages into the curriculum can enhance students' language proficiency and cultural awareness, preparing them to navigate diverse linguistic environments. Bilingual and immersion programs, in particular, offer students the opportunity to develop literacy and communication skills in more than one language, fostering cognitive flexibility and cross-cultural understanding. These programs can also empower students from minority language backgrounds by validating their linguistic and cultural identities, promoting a sense of pride and belonging.

In addition to formal education, informal language learning and cultural exchange initiatives can enrich the multilingual experience. Community language classes, cultural festivals, and language exchange programs provide platforms for individuals to engage with different languages and cultures, broadening their horizons and building connections. These initiatives can create spaces where people from diverse backgrounds come together to share their stories, traditions, and experiences, strengthening the social fabric of multilingual societies.

Technology has emerged as a valuable ally in facilitating communication and cultural exchange in multilingual societies. Digital platforms and tools enable individuals to access language resources, connect with speakers of different languages, and participate in global conversations. Social media, in particular, offers a space for individuals to share cultural content, engage in dialogues, and build virtual communities that transcend geographical boundaries. While technology can enhance language learning and cultural exchange, it is essential to ensure that digital spaces remain inclusive and accessible to all linguistic communities.

The economic and cultural benefits of multilingual societies are significant. Linguistic diversity can contribute to economic growth by attracting tourism, fostering international trade, and enhancing global competitiveness. Multilingual individuals have the ability to navigate diverse markets, negotiate across cultural boundaries, and build relationships with partners from different linguistic backgrounds. Additionally, the cultural richness of multilingual societies can attract creative industries, inspiring artistic expression and innovation.

Despite these benefits, multilingual societies must also contend with issues of linguistic inequality and discrimination. Language hierarchies can emerge, where certain languages are privileged over others, leading to the marginalization of minority languages and their speakers. Addressing these inequalities requires concerted efforts to promote linguistic diversity and inclusivity, ensuring that all languages and cultures are respected and valued.

Ultimately, multilingual societies offer a microcosm of the global experience, reflecting the complex interplay of language, culture, and identity. They challenge us to embrace linguistic diversity as a source of strength and enrichment, encouraging us to engage with different perspectives and learn from one another. By fostering environments where multilingualism and cultural exchange thrive, we can build more inclusive and harmonious societies that celebrate the richness of human diversity.

Chapter 5: Traditions, Rituals, and the Preservation of Culture

The Importance of Rituals in Cultural Continuity

Rituals are the living threads that weave together the cultural tapestry of human societies, serving as vital conduits for transmitting traditions, values, and collective identity across generations. These structured, symbolic actions are deeply embedded in the fabric of daily life, encompassing a wide array of practices that range from religious ceremonies and communal celebrations to personal rites of passage. The importance of rituals in cultural continuity cannot be overstated, as they play a crucial role in preserving cultural heritage and fostering a sense of belonging within communities.

Rituals are, at their core, expressions of cultural identity, providing individuals with a tangible connection to their heritage and history. Through rituals, communities reaffirm their shared values and beliefs, creating a sense of unity and cohesion. These practices often encode complex cultural narratives, encapsulating the wisdom and experiences of ancestors and ensuring that they are passed down to future generations. By participating in rituals, individuals become part of a living tradition, actively engaging in the cultural dialogue that defines their community.

One of the key functions of rituals is their role in marking significant life events and transitions. Rites of passage, such as births, marriages, and funerals, are universal rituals that acknowledge and celebrate the major milestones of human existence. These ceremonies provide a framework for individuals to navigate the changes and challenges of life, offering guidance and support during times of transition. By situating personal experiences within a broader cultural context, rituals help individuals make sense of their place in the world, reinforcing their connection to the community and its values.

Rituals also serve as powerful tools for education and socialization, transmitting cultural knowledge and norms to younger generations. Through the repetition of ritual practices, children learn about their culture's history, beliefs, and customs, internalizing the values and behaviors that are deemed important by their community. This process of enculturation ensures that cultural traditions are preserved and adapted over time, enabling communities to maintain a sense of continuity even as they evolve and change.

In many cultures, religious rituals hold a central place in the community, providing a framework for spiritual expression and connection. These rituals often involve symbolic actions, such as prayer, meditation, or offerings, that facilitate communication with the divine and reinforce the moral and ethical principles of the faith. Religious rituals can bring communities together in shared worship and reflection, fostering a sense of spiritual solidarity and purpose. Additionally, they can offer comfort and solace during difficult times, providing individuals with a sense of hope and resilience in the face of adversity.

Communal rituals, such as festivals and public celebrations, play a vital role in reinforcing social bonds and fostering a sense of belonging. These events provide opportunities for communities to come together, celebrate their shared identity, and reaffirm their cultural heritage. Festivals often involve a rich tapestry of music, dance, food, and art, showcasing the creativity and diversity of the community. By participating in these communal rituals, individuals strengthen their ties to one another and to the cultural traditions that define their community.

Rituals also have the capacity to adapt and evolve, reflecting the dynamic nature of culture and society. As communities encounter new influences and challenges, rituals can be modified or reinterpreted to remain relevant and meaningful. This adaptability ensures that rituals continue to serve as effective vehicles for cultural continuity, even in the face of change. For example, some traditional rituals may be infused with contemporary elements or adapted to accommodate new technologies, allowing them to resonate with modern audiences while preserving their core significance.

In multicultural societies, rituals can serve as bridges between different cultural groups, fostering understanding and dialogue. By sharing and participating in each other's rituals, individuals from diverse backgrounds can gain insights into different cultural perspectives, building empathy and respect. This exchange can enhance social cohesion and promote a sense of shared identity, contributing to a more inclusive and harmonious society.

Despite their enduring significance, rituals can sometimes be threatened by external forces, such as globalization, modernization, and cultural homogenization. As communities become more interconnected, there is a risk that traditional rituals may be overshadowed by dominant cultural influences, leading to a loss of cultural diversity and identity. To safeguard the continuity of rituals, it is essential for communities to actively engage with and celebrate their cultural heritage, ensuring that rituals remain vibrant and meaningful.

Efforts to preserve and revitalize rituals can take many forms, from documentation and education to community engagement and advocacy. By recording and sharing the stories and practices associated with rituals, communities can preserve their cultural heritage for future generations. Education programs that incorporate cultural rituals into the curriculum can foster pride and awareness among young people, encouraging them to embrace their cultural identity. Community initiatives that celebrate and promote rituals, such as festivals, workshops, and exhibitions, can create spaces where cultural heritage is valued and shared.

Festivals and Their Role in Cultural Expression

Festivals are vibrant celebrations that pulse with life and color, offering a vivid expression of cultural identity and community spirit. They are moments when the everyday is transformed into the extraordinary, bringing people together in joyous unity. Across the globe, festivals serve as vital expressions of cultural heritage, showcasing the unique traditions, values, and creativity of diverse societies. They play a crucial role in cultural expression, providing a platform for communities to celebrate their distinctiveness while fostering a sense of belonging and continuity.

The origins of festivals are as diverse as the cultures that celebrate them. They often have roots in religious, agricultural, or historical events, marking significant milestones in the calendar year. These celebrations can range from grand, nationwide events to intimate, local gatherings, each imbued with its own customs and significance. Despite their diversity, festivals share common elements: they are communal, participatory, and imbued with meaning.

At the heart of every festival is the celebration of identity. Festivals provide a space for individuals to connect with their cultural heritage, reaffirming their sense of self and community. Through music, dance, art, and ritual, festivals express the rich tapestry of cultural narratives that define a community's identity. They offer a stage for storytelling, where the myths, legends, and histories of a people are brought to life, ensuring that these narratives are passed down to future generations.

In this communal setting, festivals become a powerful medium for cultural transmission. They are educational experiences, where participants, especially the younger generations, learn about their culture's history, values, and practices. Through active participation, individuals engage with the symbols and meanings embedded in festival activities, internalizing the cultural knowledge that is essential for cultural continuity. Whether it is the vibrant colors of Holi in India, the solemn processions of Semana Santa in Spain, or the spirited dances of the Carnival in Brazil, each element of a festival is imbued with cultural significance, offering a living lesson in heritage.

Festivals also serve as a showcase for artistic expression, providing a platform for creativity and innovation. Artists, musicians, dancers, and performers use festivals as a canvas to explore and reinterpret cultural themes, blending traditional elements with contemporary influences. This dynamic interplay between tradition and modernity ensures that festivals remain relevant and resonant, reflecting the evolving nature of culture. By celebrating artistic expression, festivals nurture creativity and inspire new generations of artists who contribute to the cultural vibrancy of their communities.

Moreover, festivals are not just cultural spectacles; they are spaces for social cohesion and community building. They bring people together, breaking down barriers and fostering a sense of unity and belonging. Through shared experiences and collective celebration, festivals strengthen social bonds and create a sense of solidarity. They offer opportunities for individuals from different backgrounds to come together, interact, and engage in dialogue, promoting mutual understanding and respect. In multicultural societies, festivals can serve as a bridge between diverse cultural groups, enhancing social harmony and inclusivity.

The economic impact of festivals is another dimension of their significance. They attract tourists and visitors, generating revenue and stimulating local economies. Festivals create opportunities for businesses, artisans, and vendors, contributing to economic development and job creation. The influx of visitors during festivals also promotes cultural exchange, as tourists engage with local traditions and customs, gaining insights into the cultural fabric of a community.

However, the commercialization of festivals can pose challenges, potentially diluting their cultural significance. As festivals grow in popularity, there is a risk that they may become commodified, losing their authentic connection to the community. To safeguard the cultural integrity of festivals, it is essential for communities to actively engage in their planning and organization, ensuring that they remain true to their roots and reflect the values and traditions they are meant to celebrate.

In recent years, festivals have also embraced sustainability, with many communities recognizing the importance of environmentally responsible practices. Efforts to reduce waste, promote eco-friendly transportation, and raise awareness about environmental issues have become integral to many festivals, reflecting a growing awareness of the need to protect the planet for future generations. By incorporating sustainability into their celebrations, festivals can serve as powerful platforms for environmental advocacy and education.

The digital age has introduced new dimensions to festival experiences, expanding their reach and accessibility. Online platforms and social media allow festivals to transcend geographical boundaries, connecting people from around the world. Virtual festivals and live-streamed events provide opportunities for global participation, enabling individuals to experience and engage with cultural expressions from afar. While digital platforms offer exciting possibilities for cultural exchange, it is important to preserve the communal and participatory essence of festivals, ensuring that they remain grounded in the shared experiences that define their cultural significance.

The Transmission of Oral Traditions

Oral traditions have long been the vibrant lifeblood of cultural heritage, serving as the primary means by which societies have preserved and transmitted their collective knowledge, values, and histories. Long before the advent of written records, oral storytelling, songs, and performances were the vehicles through which cultural wisdom was conveyed from one generation to the next. These traditions are not only a testament to the ingenuity and creativity of human societies but also a crucial component of cultural continuity and identity.

Storytelling, the most familiar form of oral tradition, is a dynamic and interactive process that engages both the teller and the listener in a shared experience. Through stories, communities pass down essential knowledge, moral lessons, and social norms, embedding them within engaging narratives that captivate and inspire. These stories often feature mythical heroes, historical events, and allegorical tales that reflect the values and aspirations of a community. As storytellers weave their narratives, they draw upon rich oral repertoires, adapting and embellishing tales to suit their audience and context, ensuring that the stories remain relevant and resonant.

Beyond storytelling, oral traditions encompass a wide array of expressive forms, including songs, chants, proverbs, and rituals. Songs and chants, often set to music, carry cultural narratives and emotions, offering a powerful means of expression and connection. Proverbs, succinct and memorable sayings, encapsulate cultural wisdom and offer guidance on various aspects of life. Rituals, with their ceremonial language and symbolic actions, reinforce communal bonds and cultural identity, marking significant events and transitions in the life of a community.

The transmission of oral traditions relies heavily on memory and oral performance, with skilled practitioners serving as the custodians of cultural knowledge. These individuals, be they griots, bards, shamans, or elders, are respected figures within their communities, entrusted with the responsibility of preserving and sharing the oral heritage. Through repetition and practice, they hone their craft, mastering the nuances of language, rhythm, and delivery that bring their performances to life. Their ability to captivate audiences and convey complex ideas through oral expression is a testament to the enduring power of the spoken word.

Despite the resilience of oral traditions, they face significant challenges in the modern world. The spread of literacy and technology has transformed the ways in which information is communicated and preserved, leading to a decline in the practice and transmission of oral traditions. As communities adopt written and digital forms of communication, the role of oral traditions in daily life may diminish, threatening the continuity of cultural heritage. Additionally, the pressures of globalization and cultural homogenization can erode linguistic diversity, further endangering oral traditions that are tied to specific languages and dialects.

Efforts to preserve and revitalize oral traditions are essential for maintaining the rich tapestry of cultural diversity that they represent. Documentation and recording of oral traditions, through audio and video media, can help safeguard these invaluable cultural resources for future generations. By capturing the voices and performances of skilled practitioners, communities can create archives that serve as repositories of cultural knowledge and inspiration.

Education and community engagement play a crucial role in the revitalization of oral traditions. Programs that incorporate oral traditions into the curriculum can foster an appreciation for cultural heritage among young people, encouraging them to engage with and participate in these practices. Workshops, festivals, and cultural events provide opportunities for communities to celebrate and share their oral traditions, creating spaces where cultural expression is valued and nurtured.

The adaptability of oral traditions is one of their greatest strengths, allowing them to evolve and thrive in changing contexts. By embracing contemporary influences and incorporating new elements, oral traditions can remain relevant and meaningful in the modern world. This dynamic interplay between tradition and innovation ensures that oral traditions continue to resonate with audiences, offering insights and inspiration that transcend time and place.

In multicultural societies, oral traditions serve as bridges between diverse cultural groups, fostering understanding and dialogue. By sharing and experiencing each other's oral traditions, individuals from different backgrounds can gain insights into different cultural perspectives, building empathy and respect. This exchange can enhance social cohesion and promote a sense of shared identity, contributing to a more inclusive and harmonious society.

Ultimately, the transmission of oral traditions is a testament to the enduring power of human creativity and expression. As living embodiments of cultural memory, they connect us to our past, inform our present, and inspire our future. By honoring and celebrating oral traditions, we ensure that the voices of our ancestors continue to echo through time, enriching our lives with the wisdom and beauty of diverse cultural expressions.

The Challenges of Preserving Cultural Heritage

Preserving cultural heritage is a complex endeavor, fraught with numerous challenges that span social, economic, and environmental dimensions. Cultural heritage encompasses both tangible artifacts and intangible traditions, each carrying the stories and identities of communities. As societies evolve and face new pressures, the task of safeguarding this heritage becomes increasingly urgent and intricate.

One of the foremost challenges in preserving cultural heritage is the relentless march of globalization. As cultures become more interconnected, there is a tendency towards homogenization, where dominant cultures overshadow local traditions. This can lead to the erosion of unique cultural identities, as communities adopt more widespread practices and values at the expense of their own heritage. The allure of modernization and the perceived benefits of aligning with global norms often tempt communities to abandon traditional practices, risking the loss of invaluable cultural knowledge.

Urbanization and development further compound this issue. As cities expand and infrastructure projects proliferate, historical sites, monuments, and landscapes are often threatened or destroyed. The pressure to accommodate growing populations and economic activities can lead to the prioritization of development over preservation, with cultural heritage sites being sacrificed for new roads, buildings, or industries. This results not only in the physical loss of heritage but also in the disruption of the cultural landscape that gives communities their sense of identity and continuity.

Economic constraints also pose significant barriers to the preservation of cultural heritage. Many communities, particularly in resource-limited settings, struggle to allocate sufficient funds for conservation efforts. The maintenance of historical sites, restoration of artifacts, and support for traditional practices require substantial financial investment, which may be beyond the reach of local governments or organizations. This financial shortfall can lead to neglect and deterioration of cultural heritage, as communities are unable to afford the necessary measures to protect and sustain their cultural assets.

Environmental factors, including climate change, further threaten cultural heritage. Rising sea levels, extreme weather events, and changing climate patterns can have devastating effects on heritage sites and traditional ways of life. Coastal regions, in particular, face the risk of losing historical landmarks to erosion and flooding, while communities dependent on specific environmental conditions for their cultural practices may find their traditions disrupted by climate shifts. The impact of these environmental changes necessitates a proactive and adaptive approach to preservation, one that anticipates and mitigates potential threats.

Political instability and conflict present additional challenges, as cultural heritage often becomes collateral damage in times of turmoil. Armed conflicts and political upheaval can lead to the deliberate destruction of cultural sites, as they are targeted for their symbolic value or become casualties of broader violence. The looting and illicit trafficking of cultural artifacts during such times further exacerbate the issue, depriving communities of their heritage and dispersing their cultural artifacts across the globe.

The preservation of intangible cultural heritage, such as languages, rituals, and oral traditions, faces its own set of challenges. As younger generations become increasingly detached from traditional practices, there is a risk of these intangible elements fading into obscurity. Factors such as migration, urbanization, and changing lifestyles contribute to the decline in the transmission of cultural knowledge, as communities adapt to new environments and circumstances. This loss of cultural continuity can weaken the social fabric of communities, as shared practices and values that bind individuals together diminish over time.

Despite these formidable challenges, there are strategies and initiatives that can support the preservation of cultural heritage. Community involvement is paramount, as local communities are the custodians of their own heritage. Empowering communities to take an active role in preservation efforts ensures that cultural heritage remains relevant and meaningful to those it represents. This can be achieved through participatory approaches that involve community members in decision-making processes, conservation activities, and the documentation of cultural practices.

Education and awareness-raising are equally important in fostering a sense of pride and responsibility towards cultural heritage. By integrating cultural education into the curriculum, young people can develop an appreciation for their heritage and a commitment to its preservation. Public awareness campaigns, cultural festivals, and media initiatives can also highlight the value of cultural heritage, encouraging broader societal support for preservation efforts.

International cooperation and partnerships can provide critical resources and expertise for preservation initiatives. Organizations such as UNESCO play a vital role in promoting the protection of cultural heritage through conventions, guidelines, and funding programs. Collaborative efforts that bring together governments, NGOs, cultural institutions, and local communities can enhance the effectiveness of preservation strategies, leveraging diverse perspectives and resources to address complex challenges.

Technological advancements offer new tools for the preservation and documentation of cultural heritage. Digital technologies, such as 3D scanning, virtual reality, and geographic information systems, enable the detailed recording and analysis of heritage sites and artifacts. These technologies can facilitate restoration efforts, create digital archives, and enhance public access to cultural heritage, ensuring that it remains accessible and engaging for future generations.

Adaptive management approaches, which incorporate flexibility and responsiveness to changing conditions, are essential for addressing the dynamic challenges of cultural heritage preservation. By monitoring and evaluating preservation efforts, communities and organizations can adjust their strategies to reflect emerging threats and opportunities, ensuring that cultural heritage remains resilient in the face of change.

Adaptive Practices in Modern Traditions

Modern traditions are living entities, constantly evolving to reflect the dynamic nature of human societies. As cultures interact and environments change, adaptive practices emerge, allowing traditions to remain relevant and vibrant. This adaptive quality is essential for the survival of cultural practices, enabling them to resonate with contemporary audiences while preserving their core values and significance.

One of the most compelling aspects of adaptive practices in modern traditions is their ability to bridge the gap between the past and the present. By incorporating contemporary elements into traditional practices, communities create a dialogue between generations, ensuring that cultural heritage is not only preserved but also invigorated. This synthesis of old and new can be seen in various forms, from the fusion of traditional and modern music to the reinterpretation of ancient rituals in contemporary contexts.

In the realm of performing arts, adaptive practices have given rise to innovative expressions that captivate and engage audiences. Traditional dance forms, for example, have been revitalized through the incorporation of modern choreography and music, creating performances that appeal to diverse audiences. By blending traditional movements with contemporary influences, dancers can explore new themes and narratives while honoring the cultural roots of their art.

Similarly, traditional music has embraced adaptive practices, resulting in vibrant new genres that reflect the cultural diversity of the modern world. Musicians often fuse traditional instruments and melodies with contemporary sounds, creating a rich tapestry of musical expression that transcends cultural boundaries. This fusion not only expands the reach of traditional music but also fosters cross-cultural collaboration and understanding.

Adaptive practices are also evident in the realm of festivals and celebrations, where communities have reimagined traditional events to reflect contemporary values and priorities. For instance, many festivals have integrated themes of environmental sustainability and social justice, aligning traditional celebrations with modern concerns. By incorporating initiatives such as waste reduction, renewable energy, and inclusivity, festivals can engage with pressing global issues while maintaining their cultural significance.

In the culinary world, adaptive practices have led to the creation of new dishes and flavors that reflect the changing tastes and dietary preferences of modern societies. Chefs and home cooks alike have embraced the challenge of reinterpreting traditional recipes with contemporary ingredients and techniques. This culinary innovation not only keeps traditional cuisines relevant but also celebrates the creativity and adaptability of cultural practices.

Adaptive practices extend beyond artistic and culinary expressions, influencing the way communities approach rituals and ceremonies. As societies become more diverse and interconnected, traditional rituals may be adapted to accommodate different cultural perspectives and beliefs. This inclusivity ensures that rituals remain meaningful and accessible to all members of a community, fostering a sense of unity and belonging.

In the realm of language, adaptive practices play a crucial role in ensuring the survival of endangered languages and dialects. Language revitalization efforts often involve the creation of new words and expressions to reflect contemporary realities, enabling speakers to engage with modern concepts while preserving linguistic heritage. Technology has also become a valuable tool in language preservation, with digital platforms and resources facilitating the documentation and teaching of traditional languages.

The adaptability of traditional crafts and artisanal practices is another testament to the resilience of cultural heritage. Artisans have embraced new materials, tools, and techniques to create innovative products that appeal to modern consumers. By balancing tradition with innovation, craftspeople can sustain their livelihoods while preserving the skills and knowledge passed down through generations.

In educational contexts, adaptive practices have been instrumental in integrating cultural heritage into modern curricula. Schools and educational institutions have developed programs that blend traditional knowledge with contemporary learning methods, providing students with a holistic understanding of their cultural heritage. This approach not only fosters cultural pride and awareness but also equips students with the skills to navigate the complexities of the modern world.

Amidst these adaptive practices, it is essential to recognize the importance of community involvement and agency. Successful adaptation requires the active participation of community members, who must have a voice in shaping the evolution of their traditions. By engaging in dialogue and collaboration, communities can ensure that adaptive practices remain true to their cultural values and aspirations.

The role of technology in facilitating adaptive practices cannot be understated. Digital platforms, social media, and online communities provide new opportunities for cultural exchange and innovation. Virtual spaces enable individuals to share and explore traditional practices from around the world, fostering a global dialogue that enriches cultural expression. At the same time, technology allows for the preservation and documentation of cultural heritage, ensuring that traditional knowledge is accessible to future generations.

While adaptive practices hold great promise for the preservation and revitalization of cultural heritage, they also present challenges that must be navigated with care. The balance between tradition and innovation requires thoughtful consideration, as communities strive to maintain the integrity and authenticity of their cultural practices. Ensuring that adaptive practices are inclusive and respectful of diverse perspectives is essential for fostering a sense of ownership and pride in cultural heritage.

Chapter 6: Cultural Influences on Art and Expression

The Relationship Between Culture and Art

Culture and art are intricately entwined, each reflecting and shaping the other in a continuous dance of expression and identity. Art serves as both a mirror and a beacon for cultural values, beliefs, and experiences, offering insight into the collective psyche of societies. Through various forms—whether music, visual arts, literature, or performance—art captures the essence of cultural narratives, providing a powerful medium for storytelling and communication.

Artistic expression is deeply rooted in the cultural context from which it emerges. It draws upon the symbols, languages, and traditions of its environment, creating works that resonate with the shared experiences and histories of a community. This connection imbues art with cultural significance, allowing it to convey complex ideas and emotions that transcend verbal language. Through art, cultures articulate their values and worldviews, offering a glimpse into the diverse tapestry of human experience.

In many ways, art functions as a cultural repository, preserving the heritage and identity of a people. Historical artworks, for instance, offer invaluable insights into the customs, attire, and social structures of past societies. By studying these works, we can piece together the narratives of those who came before us, understanding their triumphs, struggles, and aspirations. This preservation of cultural memory is vital for maintaining a sense of continuity and identity, allowing future generations to connect with their roots.

Art also plays a transformative role in shaping cultural identity. It not only reflects existing cultural norms but also challenges and redefines them. Artists often serve as cultural commentators, using their work to critique societal issues and provoke dialogue. Through their creative vision, they can inspire change, encouraging societies to re-evaluate their values and beliefs. This dynamic interplay between art and culture fosters an environment of growth and evolution, where new ideas can take root and flourish.

The relationship between culture and art is particularly evident in the way cultural diversity influences artistic expression. Different cultural groups bring their unique perspectives and traditions to the artistic landscape, enriching it with a multitude of styles and forms. This diversity of expression celebrates the richness of human creativity, allowing for a cross-pollination of ideas and techniques. As cultures interact and exchange artistic influences, new hybrid forms emerge, reflecting the interconnectedness of our global community.

In contemporary society, the role of art as a cultural bridge has become increasingly significant. In an era of rapid globalization and technological advancement, art offers a means of fostering understanding and empathy among diverse cultural groups. Through exhibitions, performances, and digital platforms, individuals can engage with the art of other cultures, gaining insight into different ways of life and perspectives. This cultural exchange promotes mutual respect and appreciation, enhancing social cohesion and inclusivity.

Artistic movements throughout history have often been driven by cultural and political contexts, illustrating the profound impact of societal change on creative expression. The Renaissance, for example, was a period of unprecedented artistic flourishing, fueled by a renewed interest in classical learning and humanism. Similarly, the Harlem Renaissance was a cultural and artistic explosion that celebrated African American identity and creativity, challenging racial stereotypes and advocating for social and political change.

In times of social upheaval and conflict, art has served as a powerful tool for resistance and healing. Artists have used their work to document oppression, express dissent, and envision a more just and equitable world. Through their creative expression, they have given voice to marginalized communities, highlighting their struggles and aspirations. Art has the capacity to transcend boundaries, uniting people in a shared vision of hope and resilience.

The economic dimension of the relationship between culture and art cannot be overlooked. Cultural industries, encompassing art, music, film, and literature, contribute significantly to economic development and job creation. They attract tourism, stimulate local economies, and foster innovation and entrepreneurship. By investing in the arts, communities can harness their cultural assets to drive economic growth and enhance quality of life.

Moreover, art education plays a crucial role in nurturing cultural awareness and creativity. By integrating art into educational curricula, students can develop an appreciation for cultural diversity and a deeper understanding of their own identity. Art education fosters critical thinking, empathy, and collaboration, equipping students with the skills to navigate an increasingly complex and interconnected world.

As we consider the future of the relationship between culture and art, it is essential to recognize the importance of preserving cultural heritage while embracing innovation. The digital age has opened new avenues for artistic expression and cultural exchange, offering unprecedented opportunities for creativity and collaboration. However, it also poses challenges, such as the commodification of art and the risk of cultural homogenization. By supporting diverse artistic voices and fostering inclusive cultural spaces, we can ensure that art continues to reflect and enrich the multifaceted nature of human experience.

Evolution of Artistic Styles Across Cultures

Art is a reflection of humanity's collective journey, capturing the essence of cultural evolution across time and space. The evolution of artistic styles across cultures is a testament to the dynamic interplay of historical, social, and environmental influences that have shaped human expression. As societies have transformed, so too have their artistic expressions, each style bearing the imprint of the cultural context from which it emerged.

In the annals of history, one can trace the evolution of artistic styles through distinct periods, each characterized by its own unique aesthetic principles and techniques. The art of ancient civilizations, such as Egypt, Mesopotamia, and the Indus Valley, was deeply intertwined with religious and political structures. Monumental architecture and intricate carvings served both as expressions of divine authority and as records of societal achievements. The emphasis on symmetry, proportion, and symbolism in these early works reflects the cultural values and cosmologies of their creators.

As we move into the classical period, the art of ancient Greece and Rome reveals a shift towards naturalism and humanism. Greek sculptors and painters sought to capture the idealized human form, celebrating the beauty and potential of humanity. This focus on realism and anatomical precision laid the groundwork for future artistic developments, influencing the portrayal of the human figure for centuries to come. Roman art, with its emphasis on portraiture and public works, continued this tradition while incorporating elements from the diverse cultures within the empire.

The Byzantine and medieval periods saw a departure from classical naturalism, as religious themes dominated artistic expression. Iconography and illuminated manuscripts became prevalent, with artists prioritizing spiritual symbolism over realistic depiction. The use of vibrant colors, intricate patterns, and gold leaf in Byzantine mosaics and medieval manuscripts reflects the transcendental aspirations of these societies, seeking to convey the divine through art.

The Renaissance marked a pivotal moment in the evolution of artistic styles, as a renewed interest in classical antiquity and humanism sparked a creative revolution. Artists like Leonardo da Vinci, Michelangelo, and Raphael pushed the boundaries of technique and perspective, mastering the use of light and shadow to create depth and realism. This period also saw the rise of individualism, with artists gaining recognition and patronage as creators in their own right. The Renaissance's emphasis on scientific inquiry and exploration of the natural world profoundly influenced the development of Western art.

As we journey into the Baroque and Rococo periods, we encounter art that is characterized by grandeur, movement, and emotion. Baroque artists like Rembrandt and Caravaggio employed dramatic contrasts of light and shadow, known as chiaroscuro, to evoke intense emotional responses. In contrast, the Rococo style embraced ornate decoration and playful themes, reflecting the opulence and excess of the aristocracy. These styles, while distinct, both sought to engage the viewer's senses and emotions, creating immersive and dynamic experiences.

The advent of the Industrial Revolution heralded new artistic movements that responded to rapid societal changes. Romanticism emerged as a reaction against industrialization and rationalism, celebrating nature, emotion, and the sublime. Artists like J.M.W. Turner and Caspar David Friedrich explored themes of awe and wonder, capturing the beauty and power of the natural world. This period also saw the rise of realism, with artists like Gustave Courbet and Jean-François Millet depicting everyday life with unflinching honesty, challenging viewers to confront social issues and injustices.

As the 19th century gave way to the 20th, art underwent a seismic transformation with the emergence of modernism. Breaking away from traditional forms and conventions, modernist artists sought to explore the inner workings of the human mind and the complexities of modern life. Movements such as Impressionism, Cubism, and Surrealism redefined artistic expression, pushing the boundaries of abstraction and experimentation. Artists like Claude Monet, Pablo Picasso, and Salvador Dalí challenged perceptions and invited viewers to see the world through new lenses.

The evolution of artistic styles is not confined to the Western canon; across cultures, diverse artistic expressions have flourished, each contributing to the global tapestry of art. In Asia, traditional art forms such as Chinese brush painting, Japanese ukiyo-e, and Indian miniature painting each embody distinct cultural philosophies and aesthetics. These styles emphasize harmony, simplicity, and the relationship between humanity and nature, reflecting the enduring spiritual and philosophical traditions of their respective cultures.

In Africa, art has long been an integral part of cultural identity and social life, with styles that vary widely across regions and peoples. From the intricate beadwork and textiles of the Maasai to the bold geometric patterns of Ndebele murals, African art celebrates community, spirituality, and the connection to the land. The influence of African art on global artistic movements, particularly in the 20th century, highlights its profound impact on the evolution of artistic styles worldwide.

In the Americas, indigenous art forms such as Native American pottery, textiles, and totem carving embody the rich cultural heritage and spiritual beliefs of their creators. These art forms are deeply connected to the natural world and often serve as expressions of cultural sovereignty and resilience. The fusion of indigenous and colonial influences in Latin America has given rise to unique artistic styles that reflect the region's complex history and cultural diversity.

As we consider the evolution of artistic styles across cultures, it is essential to recognize the role of cultural exchange and hybridity in shaping artistic expression. Throughout history, trade, migration, and conquest have facilitated the exchange of ideas, techniques, and materials, leading to the emergence of new styles and innovations. This cross-cultural dialogue is evident in the art of the Islamic Golden Age, the Silk Road, and the colonial encounters of the modern era, each illustrating the transformative power of cultural interaction.

In the contemporary world, the evolution of artistic styles continues to be shaped by globalization, technology, and social change. Artists today draw inspiration from a diverse array of cultural sources, creating works that reflect the interconnected and pluralistic nature of modern society. The digital age has opened new avenues for artistic expression, enabling artists to experiment with virtual and augmented realities, digital media, and interactive installations.

The Role of Art in Cultural Critique and Commentary

Art has long served as a lens through which society examines itself, a powerful tool for cultural critique and commentary. Throughout history, artists have wielded their creativity to question norms, challenge authority, and provoke thought. This dynamic role of art as a medium for critique is deeply embedded in its ability to communicate complex ideas and emotions, often transcending the limitations of language.

In the context of cultural critique, art has the unique ability to illuminate societal issues that might otherwise remain hidden. By drawing attention to injustices, inequalities, and contradictions within a culture, artists can inspire reflection and dialogue. This critical function is evident in the works of many artists who have used their platforms to address pressing social and political concerns. For example, the paintings of Francisco Goya, with their haunting depictions of war and suffering, serve as a stark reminder of the human cost of conflict and the moral complexities of power.

Artistic commentary is not limited to explicit representations of social issues; it often operates through metaphor and symbolism, inviting viewers to engage with multiple layers of meaning. This subtlety allows artists to explore themes that may be controversial or sensitive, offering a space for contemplation and interpretation. Consider the work of Rene Magritte, whose surreal paintings challenge perceptions of reality and identity, prompting viewers to question the nature of existence and the constructs of society.

The power of art to critique and comment on culture is amplified by its accessibility and universality. Art transcends linguistic and cultural barriers, enabling it to reach diverse audiences and provoke global conversations. Street art and graffiti, for instance, have emerged as potent forms of public commentary, transforming urban landscapes into canvases for social and political discourse. Artists like Banksy use the streets as a platform to challenge authority and highlight societal hypocrisies, engaging passersby in a dialogue about the world around them.

In literature, writers have used narrative and character to explore cultural critique, weaving stories that reflect and question the values of their time. Novels such as George Orwell's "1984" and Aldous Huxley's "Brave New World" offer dystopian visions that critique contemporary society, warning against the dangers of totalitarianism and technological control. Through the lens of fiction, these works encourage readers to reflect on the trajectory of their own societies, considering the implications of unchecked power and conformity.

The role of art in cultural critique also extends to music and performance, where artists use rhythm, lyrics, and movement to comment on social and cultural issues. Music genres like hip-hop and punk have historically been vehicles for marginalized voices, offering a platform to address systemic injustice, inequality, and resistance. Performance artists, too, challenge societal norms and expectations, using their bodies and actions to confront issues of identity, gender, and power.

Artistic movements often arise in response to cultural and political climates, with periods of upheaval and change giving rise to new forms of expression. The 20th century, in particular, witnessed a proliferation of movements that sought to critique and redefine cultural norms. From the dadaists' rejection of traditional aesthetics in the wake of World War I to the civil rights-inspired works of the Harlem Renaissance, artists have continually pushed the boundaries of form and content to reflect the complexities of their environments.

In contemporary society, the role of art in cultural critique is increasingly intertwined with technology and digital media. Artists now have unprecedented access to global platforms through which they can disseminate their work and engage with audiences. Social media, in particular, serves as a powerful tool for artistic commentary, enabling artists to reach vast audiences and participate in real-time cultural conversations. This digital landscape has democratized the dissemination of art, allowing emerging voices to contribute to cultural critique and shaping the discourse in new and innovative ways.

Despite its potential for social impact, art's role in cultural critique is not without challenges. The commercialization of art can sometimes dilute its critical edge, as market forces prioritize profit over provocative content. Additionally, censorship and political repression can limit artists' ability to express dissenting viewpoints, stifling the potential for art to serve as a catalyst for change. Navigating these challenges requires artists to balance their creative integrity with the realities of the cultural and economic landscape.

The educational dimension of art further underscores its role in cultural critique. Art education fosters critical thinking and empathy, equipping individuals with the tools to analyze and engage with cultural narratives. By encouraging students to explore diverse perspectives and question assumptions, art education cultivates a generation of thinkers and creators who are attuned to the complexities of their world.

Institutions, too, play a crucial role in supporting art as a medium for cultural critique. Museums, galleries, and cultural organizations can serve as platforms for diverse voices, curating exhibitions and programs that challenge dominant narratives and highlight underrepresented perspectives. By fostering an environment of openness and dialogue, these institutions can amplify the impact of artistic critique, encouraging audiences to engage with the issues that shape their lives.

In reflecting on the role of art in cultural critique and commentary, it is essential to recognize the agency and autonomy of artists as creators and commentators. Artists have the capacity to shape cultural narratives, offering alternative visions and challenging the status quo. By harnessing the power of art to illuminate and interrogate, they contribute to a more informed and conscious society.

Globalization's Impact on Artistic Expression

Globalization has ushered in an era of unprecedented connectivity, facilitating the exchange of ideas, cultures, and artistic expressions across the globe. This interconnectedness has profoundly impacted the way art is created, consumed, and understood, leading to a dynamic interplay of influences that shape contemporary artistic landscapes. While globalization has opened new avenues for creativity and collaboration, it has also presented challenges that artists must navigate in their pursuit of authentic expression.

One of the most significant impacts of globalization on artistic expression is the increased accessibility to diverse cultural influences. Artists today have the opportunity to explore and incorporate elements from a multitude of traditions, styles, and philosophies, resulting in a rich tapestry of hybrid forms. This blending of influences can lead to innovative works that transcend cultural boundaries, offering fresh perspectives and challenging conventional notions of identity and authorship.

The ease of travel and communication has facilitated cross-cultural collaborations, allowing artists from different backgrounds to work together and share their unique viewpoints. These collaborations can result in the fusion of techniques and ideas, fostering a spirit of experimentation and pushing the boundaries of traditional artistic practices. For instance, musicians might blend African rhythms with Western electronic elements, creating a genre that speaks to a global audience while honoring its diverse roots.

Digital technology has played a crucial role in globalization's impact on art, providing artists with platforms to reach audiences worldwide. Social media, streaming services, and online galleries offer instant access to a vast array of artistic content, allowing artists to share their work with a global audience and gain recognition beyond their local communities. This democratization of art dissemination has empowered emerging artists to showcase their talents and connect with like-minded individuals, regardless of geographical constraints.

However, the global reach of digital platforms also raises questions about authenticity and cultural appropriation. In a world where artistic influences are readily accessible, the line between inspiration and appropriation can become blurred. Artists must be mindful of the cultural contexts from which they draw, ensuring that their work respects and acknowledges the origins of the elements they incorporate. This awareness is essential for fostering genuine cross-cultural dialogue and avoiding the pitfalls of superficial or exploitative practices.

The proliferation of global artistic influences has also led to the emergence of new aesthetic trends that reflect the interconnectedness of the modern world. Contemporary art often features themes of migration, identity, and belonging, as artists grapple with the complexities of a globalized society. These themes resonate with audiences who are themselves navigating the challenges and opportunities of a world in flux, creating a shared experience that transcends cultural boundaries.

While globalization has expanded the horizons of artistic expression, it has also introduced challenges related to cultural homogenization and the erosion of local traditions. The dominance of certain cultural narratives and artistic styles, particularly those from Western media, can overshadow indigenous and minority voices, leading to a loss of diversity in artistic expression. Artists and cultural institutions must actively work to preserve and promote local traditions, ensuring that the unique cultural identities of communities are celebrated and sustained.

In response to these challenges, there has been a growing movement to decolonize art and reclaim cultural narratives. Artists are increasingly exploring themes of heritage, identity, and resistance, using their work to assert cultural sovereignty and challenge dominant narratives. This reclamation of cultural space is essential for maintaining the vibrancy and diversity of artistic expression in a globalized world.

The economic dimension of globalization also impacts artistic expression, as the art market becomes increasingly international. Artists and galleries must navigate the complexities of global commerce, balancing the demands of a competitive market with the desire for creative authenticity. The commercialization of art can lead to the prioritization of marketable styles and themes, potentially stifling innovation and marginalizing non-commercial voices. To address this, artists and cultural organizations must advocate for diverse funding models and support systems that prioritize artistic integrity and diversity.

Education plays a vital role in equipping artists to navigate the globalized landscape. Art education programs that emphasize cross-cultural understanding and collaboration can empower artists to engage with global influences in a thoughtful and informed manner. By fostering an appreciation for diversity and encouraging critical reflection, these programs can prepare artists to contribute meaningfully to the global artistic community.

Institutions, too, must adapt to the realities of globalization, curating exhibitions and programs that reflect the richness and complexity of the global artistic landscape. By showcasing diverse voices and perspectives, museums and galleries can facilitate cultural exchange and dialogue, enriching the experience for audiences and artists alike. This commitment to inclusivity and diversity is essential for ensuring that the art world reflects the interconnected nature of contemporary society.

In reflecting on globalization's impact on artistic expression, it is clear that the benefits and challenges are deeply intertwined. The increased connectivity and exchange of ideas have the potential to enrich artistic expression and foster a more inclusive and dynamic cultural landscape. However, artists and cultural institutions must remain vigilant in preserving the diversity and authenticity of artistic voices, ensuring that the globalized art world reflects the full spectrum of human creativity.

Globalization offers an opportunity for artists to engage with a broader audience and explore new forms of expression, but it also demands a commitment to cultural sensitivity and equity. By embracing the richness of global influences while honoring the unique contributions of local traditions, artists can create works that resonate with audiences worldwide and contribute to a more connected and understanding world.

Case Studies of Cross-Cultural Artistic Collaborations

Cross-cultural artistic collaborations offer a fascinating glimpse into the creative potential that emerges when diverse perspectives and traditions converge. These collaborations not only enrich the artistic landscape but also foster deeper understanding and connection between cultures. Through a series of case studies, we can explore how artists from different backgrounds have united their talents to produce works that transcend boundaries and challenge conventional narratives.

One notable example of cross-cultural collaboration is the partnership between Japanese artist Yayoi

Kusama and Western pop artist Andy Warhol in the 1960s. Although they never formally collaborated on a single work, their mutual influence and the dialogue between their styles exemplify the power of cross-cultural exchange. Kusama's polka dots and repetitive patterns resonated with Warhol's exploration of consumer culture and mass production. Both artists engaged in a visual conversation that blurred the lines between East and West, high art and commercialism, ultimately redefining the landscape of contemporary art.

In the realm of music, the collaboration between Indian sitar virtuoso Ravi Shankar and American musician George Harrison of The Beatles stands as a landmark moment in cross-cultural artistic exchange. Shankar's influence on Harrison not only introduced the sounds of Indian classical music to a global audience but also sparked a broader interest in Eastern spirituality and philosophies. Their partnership, highlighted by performances such as the Concert for Bangladesh, showcased the harmonious fusion of Indian and Western musical traditions, inspiring countless artists to explore the possibilities of cross-cultural collaboration.

The world of dance offers another compelling example with the collaboration between American choreographer Martha Graham and Japanese dancer Eiko Otake. Their partnership brought together Graham's modern dance techniques with Otake's Butoh-inspired movement, creating performances that explored themes of identity, transformation, and cultural displacement. This fusion of styles challenged traditional notions of dance, emphasizing the fluidity and adaptability of artistic expression across cultural boundaries.

In literature, the collaborative efforts of Nigerian writer Chimamanda Ngozi Adichie and American author Zadie Smith have provided profound insights into the complexities of identity and cultural hybridity. While each writer maintains a distinct voice, their joint discussions and public dialogues have highlighted shared themes of migration, race, and belonging. Their cross-cultural exchange has not only enriched their individual works but also contributed to a broader conversation about the global dimensions of literature and storytelling.

The visual arts have also witnessed impactful cross-cultural collaborations, such as the partnership between Chinese artist Ai Weiwei and Swiss architects Herzog & de Meuron for the design of the Beijing National Stadium, famously known as the "Bird's Nest." This collaboration blended Ai Weiwei's conceptual vision with the architects' technical expertise, resulting in an iconic structure that symbolizes China's emergence on the global stage. The project exemplifies how cross-cultural partnerships can merge artistic innovation with cultural symbolism, creating works that resonate on multiple levels.

In film, the collaboration between Mexican director Guillermo del Toro and Spanish filmmaker Alfonso Cuarón has produced a body of work that transcends cultural and linguistic barriers. Both directors share a fascination with magical realism and fantastical storytelling, drawing on their Latin American heritage to create visually stunning films that explore universal themes of fear, wonder, and humanity. Their partnership, characterized by mutual support and creative exchange, has elevated their individual projects and contributed to the global recognition of Latin American cinema.

Theater, too, has seen powerful cross-cultural collaborations, such as the partnership between South African playwright Athol Fugard and British director Peter Brook. Their work on productions like "The Tempest" integrated African storytelling traditions with Western theatrical practices, challenging audiences to reconsider the boundaries of classical theater. Through their collaboration, Fugard and Brook created performances that celebrated cultural diversity while addressing the social and political complexities of post-apartheid South Africa.

These case studies illustrate the transformative potential of cross-cultural artistic collaborations. By bringing together diverse perspectives and traditions, artists can create works that resonate with audiences worldwide, transcending cultural and linguistic barriers. Such partnerships not only expand the possibilities of artistic expression but also foster a deeper understanding of the interconnectedness of human experience.

However, successful cross-cultural collaborations require careful consideration and respect for the cultural contexts from which they emerge. Artists must navigate the complexities of cultural exchange with sensitivity and awareness, ensuring that their work honors and acknowledges the contributions of all involved. This requires open communication, mutual respect, and a commitment to genuine collaboration, where all voices are valued and heard.

As global connectivity continues to increase, the opportunities for cross-cultural artistic collaborations will only grow. Artists and cultural institutions must embrace these possibilities, fostering an environment where diverse perspectives can come together to create meaningful and impactful work. By doing so, they can contribute to a more inclusive and dynamic artistic landscape, one that reflects the richness and complexity of our interconnected world.

Through the lens of these case studies, we can see that cross-cultural collaborations are not merely about blending styles or techniques; they are about bridging divides and building connections. They challenge us to look beyond our own cultural boundaries, to engage with the unfamiliar, and to celebrate the diversity of human creativity. In doing so, they remind us of the power of art to unite and inspire, offering a vision of a world where cultural differences are celebrated and embraced.

Milton Keynes UK
Ingram Content Group UK Ltd.
UKHW020859251124
3094UKWH00042B/477